Broken Glass

Sally Grindley

BLOOMSBURY

First published in Great Britain in 2008 by Bloomsbury Publishing Plc
36 Soho Square, London, W1D 3QY

A CIP catalogue record of this book is available from the British Library

ISBN 978 0 7475 8615 9

All papers used by Bloomsbury Publishing are natural,
recyclable products made from wood grown in well-managed
forests. The manufacturing processes conform to the
environmental regulations of the country of origin.

Typeset by Hewer Text UK Ltd, Edinburgh
Printed in Great Britain by Clays Ltd, St Ives Plc

3 5 7 9 10 8 6 4

www.bloomsbury.com
www.sallygrindley.co.uk

To Chris Downs – my travelling friend,
and the lovely Anthea, Bharat and Ashok Gupta

Chapter 1

We hadn't always lived on an island. We moved on to our island when I was twelve and my brother Sandeep was nine. Up until then, we would never even have dreamed of living anywhere like that. Why would anyone dream of such a thing if they had a house with its own path and a gate at the end of it? Our house had a path and a gate and two bedrooms and a kitchen, and a room that we could sit in to watch television. We didn't all have to sleep in the same room, and we didn't have to walk all the way down the road to fetch water from a standpipe like some families had to. Some days no water came from the standpipe and then the other families had to struggle all the way over to the well at the bottom of the village.

Before we moved to our island, we went to school every day, Sandeep and I, dressed up smartly in our bright white shirts and dark grey trousers, with shoes on our feet. Not everyone in our village went to school – not everyone had shoes either – but I was glad that I did because then I could look forward to a good job when I was older. Some of the children who lived nearby had never been to school. They stared at us as if we were creatures from another world when we walked past with our satchels banging up and down on our backs. Some of them made rude comments, but we just ignored them. Most of the time we felt sorry for them, because they were sent by their parents to work in the fields instead of learning how to read and write. We knew they would never have a good job if they couldn't read or write.

Appa worked for the railways back then. Early every morning, before we were awake, our father rode off on his bicycle, straight-backed and proud in his uniform, to his office above the station in the nearby town. He dealt with timetables and ticketing, an important job, Amma said, because if he got the timetables wrong there might be a catastrophic accident. In fact, there were frequent accidents, but none of them was my father's fault.

'It's attention to detail, that's what counts,' he used to say. 'If you take care with the little things, the big things will take care of themselves.'

As soon as he had left the house, Amma cleared up after his breakfast with a great clattering of pans. That was our signal to leap from our beds and run across the yard to the toilet and washbasin, before Paati woke and demanded to be helped there first: that would make us late for school because sometimes she took a very long time. Paati was my father's mother. She shared the bedroom with Sandeep and me, and we'd grown used to the chorus of nocturnal snorts that came from her corner. If we did wake up, we would lie in our bed and mimic the sounds, giggling quietly until Sandeep turned on his side, dug his chin in my shoulder and fell sound asleep again.

We ate our breakfast with Amma if Paati wasn't ready to get up, otherwise we sat on our own and tucked into rice dumplings, moong dal dhosas or, if we were really lucky, homemade jelabis which dripped syrup down our chins and sent us rushing to the kitchen sink to wipe the stickiness from our hands. Amma was a good cook, we thought, even if Paati was always complaining to Appa that everything was too spicy or too dry or too bland or too stodgy. Paati complained to Appa about a lot of other things as well. She regularly accused Amma of being 'insensitive to the needs of a sick old woman'; of failing to provide her

3

with the comforts she deserved; of ignoring the fact that she was racked with pain from her kidneys, her bunions, her arthritis, her lungs. Amma argued that nothing she did would ever be good enough in her mother-in-law's eyes, and that Paati needed a servant rather than a daughter-in-law.

'I have a husband and children to look after as well as your mother,' she said to my father more than once. 'I cannot always drop everything the minute she demands my attention.'

'She is old,' Appa replied. 'Her mind is strong but her body is letting her down and that makes her frustrated.'

'She could still make an effort to be more agreeable,' Amma said. 'She should try saying please and thank you once in a while.'

'And you should try putting yourself in her shoes,' was Appa's answer before he changed the subject.

Mostly my mother would let Paati's biting comments pass over her head. She had no wish to upset Appa, nor to push him into choosing between the two women in his life. It was hard for her, though, even I could see that, because as soon as I stopped being a sweet little toddler, Paati began to pick on me as well.

4

Only Sandeep and Appa escaped her lashing tongue. They could do no wrong as far as she was concerned. They were the heroes, Amma and I were the villains.

When Sandeep and I finished breakfast, we set off for school. Amma, though, was left on her own with Paati, and by the time we reappeared in the early afternoon the strain showed in the tightness of her lips and the deep crease between her eyebrows.

Once a month, Amma took us into the town in a taxi. It was a real treat to go into town. Many of the villagers couldn't afford the fare, but they waved goodbye to us and we waved back as though we were film stars. As soon as we arrived, we climbed the stairs to Appa's office to say hello. I liked going there, even though it was noisy and stank of sweat and was so hot you could hardly breathe. Appa had a big desk with a computer and a telephone. On the wall behind him was a huge map showing all the stations in the region. It was always covered with pins, which Appa warned us not to touch because if we did the whole rail network might come to a standstill. We never understood how moving a pin could have such an effect, but we did as we were told because we didn't dare risk making Appa angry.

There were two other desks in the office. One was

occupied by Ramit Tandon, who was sixteen, as skinny as a bean stick, and leapt like a startled rabbit every time my father ordered him to do something. He shrank into his seat the minute we opened the office door, shuffled papers in an attempt to look busy, chewed the inside of his mouth, and refused to make eye contact with us. Amma said that he had been terrified of other children ever since being bullied mercilessly at school because he was cross-eyed. I so badly wanted to see what he looked like with his eyes crossed, but not once did I manage to catch Ramit Tandon off guard.

Behind the other desk sat Naresh Kumar. He had worked for the railways for fifty-two years, and knew everything there was to know about engines and rolling stock. He only had one hand. He had lost the other when he fell from the back of his uncle's motorbike at the age of ten. Sandeep and I were fascinated by the knobbly stub that remained and by the way he used it as a prop. We were fascinated, too, by his black and broken teeth. Appa said they were rotten because of the bowl of sweets he kept on his desk, and which he held out to Sandeep and me whenever we visited. If he wasn't sucking on a sweet, a beedi dangled precariously from his mouth and bobbed up and down when he spoke. His voice sounded as though he'd swallowed a box of nails, but it was caused, Appa said, by the smoking.

Appa was always on the telephone when we arrived, shouting instructions and waving his arms around. I thought how important he must be to have two people working for him in the office and more people at the end of a telephone waiting for him to tell them what to do. I knew that when I grew up I wanted to be just as important and have people working for me, even if I did think that Appa was the most scary person in the world when he shouted.

While we waited for him to finish talking, we stood at the back of the office and looked through the window down to the station below. We never grew tired of gazing at the crowds who were gathered there in the hope that a train might soon take them to their destinations. It was like watching the whole world crammed into one small space. There were smartly dressed young men and women on their way to work. There were mothers with children and babies. There were older people setting off to visit members of their families. There were porters, taxi drivers, newspaper vendors, and hawkers of everything from silk scarves to bottled water. We could see them all from our watchtower, but hardly anyone saw our eager faces peering over the bottom of the frame.

The continuous thunder of the stationary engines was bad enough in Appa's office, but the roar from those that were just arriving or departing was brain-numbing even with the window closed. It was never open. You wouldn't have been able to think at all with it open. You wouldn't have been able to breathe at all. We could see the foul fumes from the engines rising, swirling, trying to find a way through the glass. And on the other side of the room the windows also remained firmly shut, to keep out the noise and dirt from the busy street below. Amma worried about my father's health, stuck as he was all day long in this furnace.

'You'll suffocate one day,' she was always saying, 'and nobody will know.'

'Oh, they'll know soon enough, when all the trains come to a halt,' replied my father.

'When I'm grown up, I'm going to have a great big office with windows that open out on to the sea,' I said.

'Well, you'll be the lucky one,' said my father.

'I'm going to work hard,' I said simply.

'And you think I don't,' he grimaced.

Our visits only lasted about ten minutes. There was no real purpose to them except that they allowed Appa to show us off to Naresh and Ramit and, by slipping some rupees into our hands, to show himself off as a loving and kind husband and father. When we left, we skipped alongside our mother and pestered her to be allowed to spend our rupees, which were already burning holes in our neatly pressed pockets. We stared longingly into toy shops and sports shops, and once, between us, we pooled enough money to buy a cricket bat and ball. But the ball was quickly lost and the bat split in two when we used a stone as a replacement. Mostly, all we could afford to buy was a pack of cards or an ice cream, but it was the only money our father ever gave us so, no matter how little, it always seemed like a fortune.

For the rest of our day in town, we followed my mother around as she stocked up on everything from turmeric to cotton thread to notepaper to light bulbs. Some of the things were available in our village shop, but Amma disliked the queues and having to listen to other villagers gossiping.

'They're so busy talking about other people's lives, they forget to look at their own,' she said, 'which is probably just as well because they may not like what they see.'

We loved gazing into shops at all the things we had seen advertised on television but which nobody we knew possessed. My favourites were the stores selling electrical goods like television sets that would take up half a wall in one of our rooms at home, and laptop computers that were so thin I couldn't believe they could fit anything inside them. Sandeep stood with his mouth wide open whenever we saw demonstrations of computer games, and once, when a shopkeeper allowed me to have a go on one where you had to fire at aliens from another planet, I was so excited that I couldn't have hit one even if it had taken up the whole of the screen.

'How anyone can afford such frivolities I shall never know,' my mother said, but I think she enjoyed looking almost as much as we did, especially at the clothes shops with their dazzling collections of silks and saris, and at the jewellers with their gold and diamonds.

By the time Amma had bought everything she needed and we were ready to go back home, we were loaded down with bags which banged irritatingly against our flagging legs as we tried to hire a taxi. We threw ourselves on to the seats when at last one stopped to pick us up. Within seconds Sandeep was asleep, his head bumping up and down on my shoulder, even though the driver always chattered loudly all the way to our gate.

The joy of our monthly outing was quickly snuffed out. Even as we walked up to our front door, Sandeep and I exchanged grimaces. We went through it to be greeted by Paati's disapproving scowl. Sitting in her chair in the corner of the room, her shoulders hunched and elbows pressed into her sides as though she were freezing cold, she would complain bitterly that we had no feelings if we could leave an old woman on her own for so long without so much as a glass of water. Sandeep would scamper over and lay his head on her lap. I would rush to the kitchen and fetch a drink. Amma would sigh deeply, apologise, but point out that it was necessary sometimes for her to leave the house and that it would be good for Paati to have some fresh air herself once in a while.

'Why don't you go into the village and sit in the shade with your friends?' my mother often asked. 'It will put fresh air into your lungs. You can watch the world go by.'

'Pah!' Paati snarled. 'You think these poor legs of mine can carry me that far when they cannot even take me to the kitchen? Do you think my lungs can cope with fresh air? Do you think I want to sit and listen to tittle-tattle?'

11

We all knew that Paati was quite capable of getting up and doing things for herself when there was nobody there to be at her beck and call. On Sundays, after we had all been to the temple, Appa would take her for a walk and, though she leaned heavily on a stick as she went down the path, she scarcely used it at all once she was on her way. We loved having the house to ourselves during the hours she was gone. Sandeep and I indulged in noisy play-fights, while Amma threw open the shutters to let in the light and put on her favourite radio programmes. Even when Paati returned, the atmosphere was brighter as long as Appa was around. Paati was a different person when her favourite son was there to indulge her. He remained aloof from us though. I don't think he saw it as his role to spend too much time with us, though Amma said he was deeply proud of our every small achievement at school.

Chapter 2

We escaped to our island when we could no longer cope with Appa's rages. We had learned from a very early age to tread carefully around him when a storm was brewing. The snapped response to a simple question, the demand for silence, the slammed door, the warning lights in my mother's eyes sent us scurrying to our room or out into the street. A bad day at work, the long and tiring journey home, the heat, the monsoon, the stress of having five mouths to feed, Paati's hectoring, Amma's difficulties with Paati, our own boisterousness, could all spark a sudden swing in my father's mood from rather serious and distant to fuming.

Paati was the best at controlling him at those times, but she also delighted in fanning the fire before pouring water on it. If Appa was angry at me over one thing, she would tell him of others that required his disapproval. If the monsoon was wearing him down, she would tell him that it was going to get worse before it got better. If he was worried about all the mouths he had to feed, she would tell him that two of the mouths were growing bigger every day. If he complained about his job, she asked him what he expected working in such dreadful conditions. Amma pursed her lips whilst this was happening, powerless in the face of Paati's insistence that only she knew how to handle him. She saw my father's spirits plummet, then his fury mount, and suffered the storm as well as she could, before breathing a sigh of relief once calm was restored.

When Paati died, Appa was inconsolable. It was very sudden. She had a bad fall getting out of bed one morning when, instead of asking for Amma's help, she had tried to manage on her own. We heard the bang and rushed to see what had happened, but Paati insisted she was all right and told us to stop fussing. She went back to bed and stayed there that day. By the next morning she had developed one of her coughs, but she wouldn't hear of it when Amma suggested fetching the doctor.

'When I need a little bit of help, you just ignore me,'

14

she said. 'Now that I want nothing more than to be left in peace, all you do is fuss around like a chicken in a haycart. Go about your chores and leave me be, will you?'

Paati's cough worsened and she became feverish. The only person she would allow near her was Appa. He stayed home from work and demanded that Amma bring him cold towels to lay across her forehead. Sandeep and I were sent to stay with Dipak Jangra, a friend in the village, so that we couldn't disturb her. We were happy to be away from our home, where I felt we weren't wanted and where the atmosphere was so tense we hardly dared to breathe. Three days later, Amma arrived as though to take us to school, as she had on the previous mornings, but instead she took us back to our house and told us that Paati had passed away.

I didn't know how I felt at first. The good thing was that Sandeep and I had our bedroom to ourselves, and I was relieved that there was nobody now to tell Appa that I was always doing wrong. Sandeep didn't really understand and cried for his grandmother for a while, but we both benefitted from the fact that Amma had more time for us. The bad thing was that Appa began to punish us for the pain he was suffering. Amma said that he had been devoted to his mother and that we must be patient and keep out of his way while he dealt with his grief. We tried, we tried really hard, but it was so difficult. If we disturbed his thoughts with our play or our chatter, he turned on us and accused us of having no respect for our grandmother. We began to feel that he didn't want us there at all.

'When will Appa be happy again?' Sandeep asked Amma one day when we were walking round the fields near the village.

'When he sees that his life is still blessed with many good things and can learn to smile on them again,' Amma replied.

'When will that be?' asked Sandeep.

'Soon,' Amma said, but there was a melancholy in her voice which made me wonder if she believed it.

Appa didn't go back to work straight away, and in the confines of our house he was like a tiger in a cage. He paced from room to room, and stood motionless by the chair that Paati used to occupy, as if expecting her to return. When at last Amma managed to persuade him that he would feel better if he kept himself occupied, he rode off one morning on his bicycle, but the straight back had gone and his uniform no longer seemed to fit him.

He returned that day with a bottle of whisky and started to drink. He had never touched alcohol before, calling it the nectar of the weak. Now, when he poured himself a fourth glass, Amma put her hand gently on his shoulder and pleaded with him to stop. He leapt from his chair and pushed her angrily away.

'Am I to have no comfort?' he snarled. 'Leave me be, woman, and take those brats out of my sight.' He emptied the glass in one go and slammed it down on the table.

Amma was so shocked she couldn't move. I took Sandeep's hand and led him from the room as my father slumped back down in his chair. Looking round, I saw that my mother was still standing in the same place, unsure of what to do. I hovered anxiously by the door, until she waved me away. I sat on the bed in our bedroom, hoping that she might come and see us. I wanted to put my arms round her and tell her that I loved her. There was no sound for what seemed like minutes on end.

'What's happening?' Sandeep asked.

I told him to hush. We listened and heard raised voices. Suddenly, I was afraid for my mother's safety. I crept back out into the hallway and listened. My parents were arguing but I couldn't make out the words. After a while their voices quietened down. I thought there was a sound of someone crying, but I wasn't sure. We stayed in our bedroom after that, then took ourselves to bed.

Just as we were falling asleep, Amma came to wish us goodnight. She told us how sorry my father was for what he had said.

'Doesn't Appa love us any more?' Sandeep asked.

'Of course he does, my little tiger,' Amma replied. 'And at the weekend he is going to take us all into town to see a film.'

Sandeep leapt out of bed and threw himself into our mother's arms.

'Does he mean it, Amma?' I asked 'Are you sure he means it?' We had never been to the cinema before, because Paati had thought it unsuitable, though she insisted that Appa take her once a month. It was something I had long dreamed about. 'Of course he means it, Suresh,' my mother insisted.

Appa made a big effort over the next three days to involve himself in our lives. He even came back early from his office on one of the days, carrying with him a new cricket bat and ball. We ran to the wasteground on the edge of the village and started to play. It wasn't long before a crowd of children had gathered round, waiting for a signal to say that they could join in. I didn't think Appa would let them, but all of a sudden he gave them a thumbs-up and they rushed forward.

It was the best day of my life, standing on that stretch of dusty earth, surrounded by all the other children from the village, including my friends from school, who were whooping and shouting with joy. My father was at the centre of it all and smiling. We stayed there until the smells from a hundred suppers gnawed at our bellies and lured us back home.

'Time for some of Amma's delicious cooking,' laughed Appa. He took hold of our hands, awkwardly, and led us home.

We were all so happy sitting round the table that evening. Because Appa seemed relaxed, we could relax as well. After we had eaten, he helped Amma to wash the pans. I'd never seen him do that before. And as soon as they had finished, we sat in a big heap on the sofa in front of the television. Appa let us choose what to watch. Sandeep was desperate to see a programme about snakes. I would have preferred to watch the basketball, but I gave in because I didn't want us to fight, not when everything was so good. Appa even let us stay up late.

The next day he learned that he no longer had a job.

Chapter 3

We didn't go to the cinema, not that weekend nor any other weekend. Appa came home and told us that in a month's time the railway company was closing his office and transferring his duties to a central department. It was no reflection upon his abilities, they said, they were grateful to him for his service over the years, they were offering him three months' pay to help him while he found another employment, and they wished him well for the future.

'What do they care about my future?' Appa raged. 'What do they care that I have a family to feed? Naresh? He only has himself to worry about, and he was lucky to keep his job for so long anyway, the shiftless crud-sucker. Ramit? He's young, he'll find something else, and if not he can run home to his mother. Me? Where will I find work at my age when every suitable position has a queue a mile long to fill it?'

Amma tried to reason with him that with his skills he would be able to move to the front of any queue, but Appa was adamant that he had been dealt a fatal blow from which he would never recover. He poured himself a large drink and sank into a chair.

I followed Amma into the kitchen when she went to prepare our evening meal.

'Appa's wrong, isn't he, Amma?' I said. 'Everyone will want to give him a job, won't they?'

'It's not easy,' my mother sighed. 'There are not enough good jobs to go round. But with your father's skills and his work record I am sure he will be inundated with offers. It's difficult for him to see that now, though. He is a proud man and his pride has been injured.'

'Will we still go to the cinema tomorrow?'

Amma gave me a hug. 'Of course we will,' she said. 'Life must go on, and didn't we promise you?'

When she mentioned it to Appa, however, saying how it would do us all good to have a day out together, he rounded on her and asked if she was completely stupid. 'I have lost my job, woman,' he growled. 'Do you think we can afford such things when there will be no money coming in?' He poured himself another drink.'

'I just thought that it would be good for us to get away from here and have a bit of fun before we have to worry too much.'

'You don't think, though, do you?' Appa sneered. 'Let me see, I am to go out and "have a bit of fun" when I have just been told that I have lost my job and, what's more, I am to have that "bit of fun" by going to the very place where I have been told that I am no longer wanted.'

I could understand that my father might not want to go anywhere near his office, but I didn't like the way he spoke to Amma.

'We promised the children,' my mother said quietly.

'Then the children will have to learn that promises get broken,' Appa retorted.

'Can we go next week?' asked Sandeep.

'One day, we'll go one day,' said Amma quickly. 'As soon as Appa has another job.'

My father snorted.

'We will go for a walk tomorrow, and perhaps we'll stop at the market and buy something nice for our supper.' Amma was desperately trying to please us, to take the sting away from Appa's harsh words and to soften our disappointment.

Even at that moment I began to think how much easier her life would be if she didn't have Sandeep and me to worry about, and how much kinder to her my father would be if we weren't there making our demands.

'I don't want to go for a walk,' said Sandeep sulkily.

'Yes you do,' I argued. 'We'll take the bat and ball and you can see how big a hit you can do.'

'I can do one so big it will hit the sun,' cried Sandeep.

'As long as you don't put it out,' smiled Amma. 'We don't want it to turn cold.'

I looked at Appa, hoping that he might be smiling too, but he had closed his eyes and seemed to have sunk even further into the chair. He didn't join us for our meal that evening. We ate in silence, afraid of disturbing him. Amma kept looking over to him to see if he stirred. He didn't.

He was still sitting in the chair the next morning when Sandeep and I raced into the room. I don't know if he had been to bed or not. He was staring straight ahead. I went over and put my hand on his shoulder. He didn't respond. Sandeep knelt down by his legs and put his head in his lap. Appa left him there for a moment, then pushed him away, not unkindly but firmly.

'Are you coming for a walk with us, Appa?' I asked him. 'We're going to take the bat and ball.'

He looked at me strangely, as if he didn't know who I was.

'Don't go bothering your father now,' ordered my mother, coming into the room just then. 'Eat your breakfast and we'll leave him in peace.'

We were pleased to leave the house, Sandeep and I, and to run down the road into the village. We stopped to watch a troupe of monkeys squabbling in the neem tree. One of them was holding an apple and was determined not to share it, while the others tried all sorts of different tactics to snatch it away. When the apple fell to the ground by our feet, the monkey shrieked and scrambled from the tree as fast as it could. It wasn't fast enough. Another monkey had been sitting in a bush watching the commotion. The minute the apple fell, it leapt from the bush, made a grab for it and hurtled away with it. The original owner arrived and screeched with fury as the thief disappeared from sight, then it took itself off to sit on a broken fence post, forlorn and defeated.

'Poor monkey,' said Sandeep.

'He looks really sad,' I added.

'Can we buy him another apple at the market?' asked Sandeep.

'I think the monkey must sort out his own problems,' said Amma.

'He won't starve, will he?' asked Sandeep.

'Only if he's not wise,' Amma said quietly. 'Come on, now, that's enough talk of monkeys. We'll fetch some food at the market then walk down to the river for tiffin. If we're lucky, we might just see the otters.'

Sandeep and I raced ahead until we reached the first market stall. We waited for Amma to catch up, then darted from one stall to another, picking up fruits and examining them on the way, stopping to breathe in the sickly smell of ghee sweets, the choking fumes of turmeric and the soothing scent of coconut. We stood and watched a man cooking poppadums and chapattis, and another who chatted with my mother as he fried batches of puris. They puffed up into little balls, which he turned with a deft flick of the wrist as soon as one side was cooked. We begged to be allowed one. Amma was going to say no, but the man picked one up for each of us and put them into our hands. We juggled them, giggling and squealing, from one hand to the other until they had cooled down, then bit greedily into them.

'Anybody would think I didn't feed you,' Amma said, shaking her head.

'You don't,' I grinned and ducked as she aimed a playful smack in my direction.

As soon as my mother had filled our tiffin baskets with enough tasty snacks we set off again. We loved going to the river. There were so many games we could play there. We would throw stones into the water and count the ripples. We adopted ducks and cheered them past an imaginary finishing line. We hurled twigs and watched to see which one would go the furthest before being caught up in undergrowth. We paddled along the shallows and peered through the water to see if we could spot any fish. We could stay there all day and never grow tired of it, especially now that a family of otters had moved in and we could hope to see them.

We reached a patch of green and made that our base. While Amma laid a cloth on the ground, Sandeep and I pushed our way through the rushes that lined the banks and scrambled down to a platform of dried mud by the water's edge. We bent over, our eyes darting backwards and forwards until Sandeep shouted, 'Fish, I saw a fish! Beat you to it!'

I looked to where he was pointing but couldn't see anything. 'You're making it up,' I accused.

'There was a fish, a big one,' Sandeep argued.

I took another step forward, tripped on a hidden root, and fell face first into the water. Sandeep hooted with laughter, then jumped in next to me, whirling his arms round and splashing me. I pushed him over and we wrestled in the water, until we both sat down exhausted.

'Well,' cried Amma, 'if there were any otters close by, they will have packed their bags and run away by now.'

'Run away, run away,' sang Sandeep. 'I saw a fish and the fish ran away.'

'Foolish boy,' I giggled. 'Fish can't run, they haven't got legs.'

'Run away, run away,' Sandeep sang on. 'I saw a foolish boy and the boy ran away.'

'I think the sun must have got to that foolish boy's head,' chuckled Amma.

'Run away, run away,' shrieked Sandeep. 'I saw the sun and the sun ran away.'

'What, did the monsoon come?' I grinned, scrambling out of the river. 'Watch out, it's coming now.' I grabbed a bowl Amma had laid on the grass, filled it with water, and tipped it over Sandeep's head. I darted back and hid behind Amma for protection. My brother jumped out and dashed towards us, then shook himself like a dog so that we were both showered with spray.

'Aargh! Shoo that mad dog away!' I ordered my mother.

'Well, I think we could tame that mad dog,' she replied. 'Lie down, good boy,' she said firmly.

Sandeep lay down on his back, his legs in the air, and began to snore.

Just then, a man came by carrying a walking stick in one hand and a bird cage in the other. Inside the cage was a small parrot.

'That's a fine snore you have there,' the man said, stroking his beard. He stopped and put the cage on the ground. 'With a snore like that you are destined to be a leader of men.'

I snorted at the thought of my little brother being a leader, especially if all it took was a snore to single him out from the rest of the world.

'And you, sir,' he continued, looking at me sharply, 'will struggle to make your way in life if you treat the divinations of your elders with such derision.'

I wanted to snort again, at the man's pomposity, but Amma fired me a warning glare.

'Little Sandeep is very good at his sums and he has a fine ear for language,' she said, looking fondly at my brother. 'My eldest, whose name is Suresh,' she continued, patting my hand, 'has a creative mind. At the moment he says he wants to work in an office, but one day I think he will tell the world great stories.'

I sat up straight and proud when she said that. I had never previously heard her voice her thoughts about my future. I had always thought that I would work in an office like my father. I liked the idea of being a storyteller, and wondered if I could make up a story about the funny little man who stood before us now with his parrot and his walking stick.

'What's your parrot called?' asked Sandeep.

'Anoop, he is called Anoop,' the man said, 'and my name is Dakshesh Dahliwal. If you like he can tell you your fortune.'

'My husband has lost his job, Mr Dahliwal. We cannot afford such frivolities,' my mother said firmly.

'Madam, you cause me great insult by choosing to describe our calling as a frivolity.'

'I don't mean to insult you, sir, and I am sure you are a champion of your craft.' I could see that Amma was irritated by the man's presence and wanted him to leave us in peace, but I wanted to hear the parrot tell our fortunes, and to know what he would say about mine.

'Please, Amma,' I begged. 'Please let him.'

'I have an idea,' Dakshesh Dahliwal said. 'I like you all very much, so I will tell all your fortunes but only charge you for one.'

'No, thank you,' said Amma, but her voice had lost its resolve. Perhaps she was curious too. The man had already begun to scatter a bunch of handmade cards with writing on one side on to the ground in front of us.

'You will see,' he said. 'Anoop cannot wait to do his job. It is his destiny to help you to look into the future.'

The parrot was strutting restlessly from one side of its cage to the other, stopping to bite at the wire walls and cocking its head at its master. When Dakshesh Dahliwal opened the door at last, the parrot hopped out, turned towards the display of cards, rocked backwards and forwards, then picked up a card in its beak. It held it for a moment, then dropped it and chose another one.

'Whose fortune is he going to tell?' I asked.

'He doesn't know, that's why he dropped the card.'

'Me first,' cried Sandeep. 'I want to go first.'

'Sit here, then.' Dakshesh Dahliwal pointed to the ground in front of him. Sandeep shuffled forward eagerly. The fortune teller said something incomprehensible to his bird. The bird squawked something incomprehensible in reply, then hopped round and across the cards, picked one up, dropped it, picked up another, dropped it, picked up another and handed it to its master.

'What does it say, what does it say?' squealed Sandeep.

The fortune teller fed a peanut to the bird, which headed back into its cage. He studied the card. His face was very serious. He gazed at Sandeep and looked as if he was about to speak, then lowered his eyes again.

'Enough of this,' Amma said uneasily. 'We will make our own future. We don't need a bird to tell us –'

'Too late, madam,' Dakshesh Dahliwal jumped in quickly. 'Anoop has spoken already. Your son will leave you and make his own way in life, but I see that his older brother will look after him.'

'I'm not looking after him!' I cried. 'He's a pest!'

'I don't want him looking after me!' wailed Sandeep. 'He can't cook.'

'Don't be silly, you two,' Amma scolded. 'Mr Dahliwal doesn't mean *now*, and of course you will look after each other when your father and I are no longer of this world. Now, if you don't mind, Mr

Dahliwal, I will spare you some of our tiffin and this handful of rupees, but I would like you to leave us to our family day out.'

'But I haven't had my fortune told yet,' I protested.

'That will have to wait for another day,' my mother said adamantly. 'Mr Dahliwal has other people to see, and for my part I would like to enjoy the company of my sons without further interruption.'

'As you wish,' the fortune teller said testily, 'but you have not heard everything that Anoop wishes to tell you.'

'I am happy for him to keep it to himself,' Amma insisted. 'Good day to you, Mr Dahliwal.'

The fortune teller closed the door of the parrot's cage, stood up and waved his stick at my mother. 'You will miss your sons,' he warned.

'Of course I will,' my mother sighed. 'That is every mother's destiny.'

Dakshesh Dahliwal bowed slightly, gave us a tight-lipped smile and moved away.

'You upset him, Amma,' I said when he was out of earshot.

'He's a fool and a charlatan,' she replied. 'What he said could apply to anyone. I doubt whether Dakshesh Dahliwal is even his real name. If I wanted to have my

33

fortune told, I would choose my teller carefully and not put myself into the hands of any old rogue and his parrot. Now, let us put him out of our minds and enjoy the rest of our day.'

We did enjoy the rest of our day. It was fun sitting by the river tucking into the food we had bought just that morning at the market. Other families wandered by and chatted with us before continuing on their way. Sandeep and I joined in a water fight with a big group of children who had gathered a little further down the river. We didn't see any of the otters. Amma said they had probably moved to another country because of the human whirlwind that had devastated their world. We ambled back home in the late afternoon, tired, happy, and looking forward to telling Appa what we had been doing.

Chapter 4

There was no reply when we piled through the front door and called for Appa to come and greet us. Amma looked in the bedroom and through the window to the backyard, but he was nowhere to be seen.

'I expect your father has taken himself off for a walk,' she said brightly. 'A little fresh air will cheer him up.'

She began to prepare our evening meal, while Sandeep and I played dominoes on the kitchen table. An hour passed and still there was no sign of my father. Amma opened the door to see if he was coming up the road. She did the same thing every quarter of an hour after that. When another hour had gone by, an hour during which we would normally have sat down to eat, Amma said she would pop into the village to find out if anyone had seen him. She tried to sound as if she wasn't really concerned, but I could tell that she was becoming more and more worried. Appa was always there for our evening meal, and he was always prompt. It was a matter of great importance to him that we should eat together, and that we should be ready to sit down as soon as Amma called us. Sandeep had prepared the table – it was his turn – and the delicious smells that drifted from the kitchen were beginning to tease us.

When she came back, Amma shook her head, said that nobody had seen Appa since the early afternoon when he had bought a newspaper, and asked that we wait another half an hour. We waited another half an hour. By then we were so hungry that even Amma agreed that we should eat without my father.

It was so strange without him, even though he never spoke very much when he was there. He would ask us what we had been doing at school and if we were working hard. He would tell us how hard he had to work because he was saddled with one assistant who was too frightened to do anything unless he was actually told, and another who tried to get out of doing anything at all and had only kept his job for so many years because it had been given to him in the first place by a friend who was a friend of the management.

'That Naresh Kumar,' he would say more than once. 'He's a waste of what little oxygen there is circulating in the office. We'd achieve more with a baboon at his desk.'

Sandeep and I chuckled at that, but Amma thought he was being unkind because Naresh Kumar had a good heart.

'Good hearts are no good to me when I want information about a signal failure,' Appa retorted.

He left Amma to discipline us if we slurped our food or wiped our hands on the tablecloth. He would frown in our direction, waiting for Amma to notice his disapproval and act upon it. It was only when he was so angry that he couldn't hold back that he dealt with us himself.

Sitting there that evening, with the empty space where Appa normally sat, none of us spoke very much. We jumped whenever there was a noise outside, watching for the door to open. Sandeep asked if he would ever come back. Amma said that he probably needed some time and space to think about his future and that he would return when he was ready. I wondered out loud what sort of mood he would be in when he came back and whether he would like us a bit better. Amma took both our hands and said that he loved us very much, but that sometimes things went wrong in people's lives which made them unhappy or angry, and that it could seem as if they were unhappy or angry with the people they loved, even if they were not.

We had gone to bed before Appa came back. I was woken suddenly by raised voices. Sandeep was fast asleep beside me, his legs tangled round mine. I lay quietly, not wanting to disturb him. A man was talking loudly. It wasn't Appa. I tried to make out what he was saying, but Sandeep's heavy breathing blotted out some of the words and robbed them of meaning. Then I heard Appa, arguing. His voice sounded strange, rising and falling as if he had lost control of the volume. Amma said something to him. He shouted back. The other man said something else – it sounded like a warning – before I heard footsteps and the front door opening and shutting. There was silence then, apart from the noise of water running in the kitchen. I strained my ears to listen. Nothing. A few moments passed. Sandeep stirred beside me, untangled his legs and turned on to his side. I quickly rolled out of bed and tiptoed to the bedroom door.

I stood in the dark waiting – I didn't know what I was expecting – and then, through the sticky heat of the night, I heard a sound I had never heard before and one that I never wanted to hear again. It was like the agonising howl of an animal caught in a snare. In the black confines of our house it tore Sandeep from his sleep and shredded my nerves. I leapt back on to the bed and held my brother tight.

'Did something bad happen?' he murmured.

'Appa came back,' I whispered.

'Is he all right?'

I was afraid that he was far from all right. I was afraid that the strangled sobs that were now filtering through the walls meant that my father was the saddest person on earth. I was frightened that he would make Amma sad too, and then we would become the saddest family on earth. I wanted it to go quiet again. I wanted to go back to sleep and wake up in the morning and find that life had gone back to normal. I wanted Appa to have his job and I wanted him not to drink and, if it made him happy again, I even wanted Paati to be alive.

The sobbing stopped at last. Footsteps shuffled past our bedroom. The door opened and Amma peered in.

'Amma?' called Sandeep.

'Shhh, child,' Amma hushed. 'Go to sleep.'

'What's happened to Appa?' I asked.

'He's feeling unwell,' said Amma, 'but tomorrow he'll be fine again.'

'Who was the other man?'

'A friend who was kind enough to help him home. Now no more talking.'

She disappeared and at last the house fell silent.

We slept late the next morning. When we went into the kitchen, Amma had already finished cooking breakfast and was preparing vegetables for lunch.

'Where's Appa?' asked Sandeep. 'Is he better now?'

'Your father is sleeping,' said Amma, 'so try not to wake him.'

I thought he must be very ill not to be up before us on a Sunday morning. Sunday was his day for getting up early to stand in front of the mirror and trim his moustache. He liked to make sure that every single hair was precisely clipped, and to do that he required absolute peace and quiet. If by chance we did wake up and catch him in the middle of this operation, we knew from experience to creep back to our bedroom until he had finished. The day would begin badly if not. Once he was satisfied that his moustache was as it should be, he walked into the village to fetch a newspaper. He would return and sit outside on a wooden chair, a cup of chai in one hand, the newspaper in the other, reading every inch of every page until at last he closed it and went inside for breakfast. By this time we were usually ravenous and couldn't wait for Amma to appear from the kitchen carrying plates piled high with idli and coconut sauces.

That morning we ate our breakfast without Appa and we went to the temple without Appa. When we returned, he was sitting on the verandah staring into space, his hair uncombed, a dark shadow round his face.

'Are you feeling better, Appa?' I asked him.

He gazed at me for a moment, then stood up and walked into the house. Sandeep ran after him and tried to catch his hand. My father shook him away before turning back on himself, pushing past me through the door, and striding off down the path. Amma called out to him but he didn't look round and I saw the anxiety in her eyes.

'Is Appa cross with us?' Sandeep asked.

My mother shook her head. 'He's angry with the world,' she said, 'but not with you. As soon as he finds a new job, everything will be all right again.'

'You could send me to work in the fields until Appa finds something,' I said, though I hoped that the answer would be no. I didn't want to stop going to school, but if I had to I would.

Amma smiled and shook her head. 'That won't be necessary,' she said, 'and you are not even to think about missing school. It is only by going to school that one day you will have a good job like your father had and will have again. What has happened to us has happened for a reason, but we will come through it and be the stronger for it, all of us together.'

Chapter 5

Appa didn't go to work the next morning. From our room I heard him argue that since his job had been taken away from him then he had the right to take his services away from the job. 'I am not going to sit in that office while they close it down around me,' he insisted. 'Let them see how it all falls apart when I am not there.'

Amma was worried that if he didn't go they might change their minds about the three months' pay they had offered him. 'Be proud,' she said. 'Go to your work and remind them that they are losing a man of strength and integrity. You will need their kind words when you apply for another job.'

'I would rather beg in the streets than ask them for their help,' Appa stormed.

'Those are the words of a fool, and you are not a

fool,' Amma challenged. 'Think of your family if you will not go to work for yourself.'

'My family,' Appa growled. 'What a noose round a man's neck is his family.'

There was silence. It was time to get ready for school but I didn't dare move. Then the breakfast pans began to clatter, loudly, angrily. I woke Sandeep and we crept to the basin. He asked what was wrong and I told him that I didn't think Appa wanted us any more.

When we went into the kitchen, Amma was on her own. I tried to put my arms round her. She moved away and told us to hurry or we would be late. It felt like Amma didn't want us either, and I walked to school that morning full of fear for our future.

When we returned in the afternoon the house was empty. We asked our neighbours, but no one knew where Amma and Appa had gone. We changed out of our school clothes and sat down to do our homework. It was difficult to concentrate. Amma was always there when we arrived back from school, ready with bowls of yogurt and pineapple or papaya because we were always so hungry. Sandeep asked why we couldn't go and look for her, but I said that we should wait.

We waited for an hour. Sandeep sprawled in front of the television. I stood at the window and stared down the road as the light began to close in. At last, I saw two figures approaching. 'Amma,' I breathed and ran to the door. I couldn't make out who the other person was. I knew it wasn't Appa. As they drew nearer I recognised Maya Desai, one of Amma's friends. She had her arm through Amma's and seemed to be helping her along. 'Amma, what's the matter, Amma?' I cried.

'It's nothing to worry about, Suresh,' she replied breathlessly. 'I had a fall. Silly of me. Are you all right? Is Sandeep all right?'

I took her other arm and guided her into the chair on the verandah. Sandeep rushed out and put his head in her lap.

'You see what good boys I have, Maya,' she smiled, taking hold of my hand and stroking Sandeep's hair.

'Your lip is cut, Amma,' I said, 'and your eye is swollen.'

She put her fingers to her lip. They were shaking, and I saw that it caused her pain to shift in the chair.

'I'll stay with you for a while, Bindhu, until you recover your strength,' said Maya. 'Perhaps I could make preparations for your meal.'

'I'll help,' I added quickly. 'I'm good at cutting onions.'

'I'll be fine,' Amma argued, rising to her feet. 'If

everyone became incapable because of a tiny fall, then where would we be?'

I noticed the concern in Maya's face. I began to worry that Amma was more badly hurt than she was admitting.

'Where's Appa?' I asked, remembering suddenly that he hadn't gone to work.

A look passed between my mother and her friend, a look of confusion, even fear.

'Shall I go and fetch him?' I said. 'He ought to be here.'

'There's no need to bother him,' said Amma. 'He'll be back later. Now stop fussing and let me get on with our supper.'

She wouldn't hear of her friend staying any longer. I could tell that Maya was reluctant to leave, but my mother could be very stubborn. I assured her that Sandeep and I would take care of Amma and not let her overdo things. The minute she had gone, we bustled around fetching bowls, measuring out spices, cutting up onions and stirring sauces. We tried to make Amma sit down, but she said she would be sitting down soon enough once our food was cooked.

There was still no sign of Appa. When our meal was ready, Amma insisted that we eat rather than wait for him, which made me wonder if she knew where he was and that he wouldn't be coming home. I didn't feel like eating any more. My stomach was tight with anxiety. I didn't know what had happened to Amma that afternoon, but I didn't want her to be in pain, and I didn't like her being so quiet. She was shut into her thoughts, from which Sandeep and I were excluded.

When it was time for bed, Appa still hadn't returned. Sandeep snuggled up tight to me and asked if we would ever see him again. I tried to reassure him, but it was difficult because I was beginning to have doubts myself. Our father had changed so much, and our life seemed to have been thrown into turmoil. My mother's fall must have been caused by worry, I thought, and now she was sitting all alone, her face battered, her ribs bruised, wondering where her husband was and why he wasn't there with her when she needed him. I wanted to go to her, but I knew she would tell me to stop fussing again and that I needed a good night's sleep if I was to be bright for school in the morning. I couldn't sleep, though. At every small sound my ears pricked up in the hope that it was Appa. Sandeep tossed and turned by my side but he didn't wake.

It was a long time later before I heard footsteps outside and my mother whisper, 'Is that you, Ravi?'

My father's grunted reply was followed by a sound that I recognised this time. I held my breath and listened hard. Appa was sobbing. He was sobbing uncontrollably, and in between sobs he was crying, 'I'm sorry, Bindhu, I'm so sorry.' My mother's voice was soft and comforting, like it was when Sandeep grazed his knees or woke with a scream from a nightmare. I wanted to go to them, to wrap myself round them and know that everything was going to be all right. I didn't dare in case it made my father angry. I tried instead to blot out the sounds by pulling the blanket over my ears. Sandeep stirred and muttered something in his sleep. It was too hot to stay under the blanket for long, but when I pushed it back the voices in the next room had fallen silent. I heard Appa go outside. I sat up and peered through the window. I watched him settling down on the verandah, as he always did when it was too humid inside. Then I heard Amma pour herself a drink of water and go to her room.

I lay back down, closed my eyes and prayed that in the morning our life would go back to normal.

Appa had gone by the time Amma woke us up. 'Suresh, Sandeep,' she called. 'Come along, sleepy-heads, you'll be late for school.'

I jumped out of bed and ran to the basin. There was no sign on the verandah that Appa had been there, but his bicycle was missing. In the kitchen, Amma was piling pineapple and coconut dhosas on to plates while a pan of water bubbled on the stove.

'Where's Appa?' I asked anxiously as soon as I was dressed.

'Your father's gone to work,' said Amma, 'and while he is in town he will begin to look for another job.'

'He could be a policeman,' offered Sandeep. 'Policeman is a good job.'

'Are you feeling better, Amma?' I said. Her lip was swollen and her eyelid drooped. She looked tired. She looked older.

'Much better,' she smiled. 'And when your father comes home with a new job I shall swing through the trees with joy like a monkey that has found a precious fruit.'

Sandeep leapt round the room making monkey noises until Amma ordered him to sit down and eat.

'Will we be able to go to the cinema when he has his new job?' I wanted to know.

'You promised,' added Sandeep.

'If we promised then that's what we'll do,' said

Amma. 'Now hurry up, off you go and leave me in peace.'

'Will you be all right?' I turned to ask as we went through the door.

'I'll be fine. Stop worrying.'

We waved goodbye and ran off down the road.

It was only as we walked through the village that I began to sense that something was wrong. We were used to the odd stares from some of the children who didn't go to school, but that day they seemed to be whispering more than usual and pointing in our direction. Several mothers watched us as well, and when I looked back they seemed to be talking about us. I took hold of Sandeep's hand and started to walk more quickly, ignoring his protests. When we arrived at school I was sure that some of the other children, even my friends, were saying things about us. I tried to put it out of my mind and concentrate on my work, but when we stopped at midday a boy called Manek Vakil, who was older than me and from a different village, asked if my father had ever hit me. Some of the other boys looked on, waiting for my answer. I was so astonished by the question that I just stood there, until at last I managed to say, 'Of course not,' and then, more firmly, 'Of course he hasn't.'

'Just your mother,' Manek said quietly.

'My mother hasn't hit me either,' I snapped.

Someone laughed nervously. I turned to see who it was, but one of our teachers was walking towards us and everyone moved quickly away, leaving me to puzzle over what Manek had meant. I was grateful that the rest of the day passed by without any other strange things happening, and we kept our heads down as we hurried back through the village that afternoon.

As we came within sight of our house, we saw that Amma was not alone. A man was standing in the doorway. We drew closer and recognised Parth Sharma, one of the elders who dealt with problems in the village. He was talking animatedly. He stopped when Amma signalled our approach. He turned and greeted us, then immediately bade my mother farewell and marched off down the road.

'What did Mr Sharma want?' I asked when he was out of earshot.

'Nothing that need concern you,' she replied. She looked worried, though she tried to hide it by ruffling our hair and changing the subject. As soon as Appa came home, she sent us to the shop to buy some matches and a bottle of oil, even though we didn't both need to go. When we returned, my father was sitting in his chair and didn't answer when Sandeep asked if he had found a new job. I hissed at my brother to leave Appa in peace, then took him away to do our homework. We ate our evening meal in silence, while Appa stayed in his chair. I wished he would go out again, because his presence made the atmosphere dark and threatening. Our home didn't feel like home any more, and it was all his fault.

Chapter 6

Our island was like a sanctuary amongst all the noise and dirt and chaos. I couldn't believe it when I saw it and realised that nobody else lived there. Most of the places we had tried already belonged to someone else, and we were quickly told to move on as soon as we put down our bags.

We were tired, so tired, Sandeep and I, and we had scarcely eaten for two days. We had run and then walked for what seemed like miles along dusty tracks away from the village. Amma thought we were going to play cricket. She was so worn down that I think she was glad when we took ourselves off. Appa was snoring in the chair as usual, an empty bottle on the floor beside him. He wouldn't have cared anyway, I knew that. He had gone beyond caring. We were lucky when an ox cart passed close by and then stopped. We had ducked down behind a bush as soon as we heard it coming. The driver went into a field to pick some tapioca roots. While he was there, we scrambled up into the back of the cart and hid under a pile of coconut leaves. After we had gone a little way, Sandeep began to panic. He said that he couldn't breathe and that he had ants all over him and that he wanted to go home. I was scared the driver would hear him so I started to whisper the story from the Pancatantra about the foolish lion and the clever rabbit. He whimpered and I put my arm round him. I wondered if I was doing the right thing, taking him with me, but I knew that I couldn't have left him to suffer our father's violent outbursts.

We jumped out of the ox cart when it stopped in front of a house and the driver went inside. Sandeep complained that he was hungry and wanted to know when we would have our supper. All I could answer was that I would find him something as soon as possible. I hadn't a clue what, and the enormity of what I was doing paralysed me for a moment. It was beginning to grow dark, we were in the middle of nowhere, we had nothing to eat and nobody in the world to look after us. I began to think that perhaps we should have stayed and put up with the beatings.

I pushed the idea out of my head. I had to believe that Amma would be better off without us, that our absence would bring Appa to his senses. I had to keep hoping that if he didn't have to bother about us he might be kinder to Amma. And if he wasn't kinder to Amma, I had to hope that the village elders would send him away so that we could go home and look after her. I had to believe that if we went to a big town or a city I would be able to find work to feed my brother and myself. I was strong for my age, and tall. I could tell people I was sixteen and then they would be happy to employ me, especially since I could read and write and was good at maths.

I took Sandeep's arm and hurried him along the road through a small village. Several of the villagers greeted us, gazing at us curiously because we were strangers amongst them. I didn't give them time to ask questions, and slowed only when we were past all the houses and back into open country. Luckily, we came across a jack fruit that had fallen close to the roadside. We sat at the edge of a field, prised open its thick knobbly skin and sucked hungrily on the sweet juicy flesh.

'How much further have we got to go?' Sandeep asked. He licked his fingers then lay back on the ground.

'We haven't gone far enough yet,' I replied. 'We've got to catch a train first.'

He frowned and turned his head from side to side. 'I can't see any trains.'

'We've got to find a station, then we'll catch a train.'

'I'm tired,' he mumbled. He closed his eyes.

I would have liked to do the same thing myself, but I knew we had to keep going while there was still some light. 'We'll rest for ten more minu es,' I said. I lay down next to him.

'Do you think Appa will be upset that we've gone? Do you think he'll try to find us?' asked Sandeep.

'I don't know,' was all I could reply. I hoped he wouldn't try to find us.

'It really hurt when he beat you, didn't it?'

I nodded. I was glad that my eyes were closed because I could feel the pain welling up in them.

'He hurt Amma too, didn't he? She tried to be brave but I know he hurt her.'

I nodded again, by the side of that field in the middle of nowhere, not for Sandeep to see but to make myself keep in mind why we were there.

'She should leave him before he hurts her again.' Sandeep leaned across to me. 'I don't want him to hurt her again,' he said urgently.

'The village elders will protect her,' I answered.

'When will we see her again?' he asked.

'One day, when we've made enough money so that we can look after her,' I said. I jumped to my feet. 'Come on, let's go. We've got a train to catch.'

'Will there be a train in the night?'

'If not, we'll catch one in the morning.'

'If Appa was still working he could have got us a ticket,' my brother observed.

'If Appa was still working we wouldn't need a ticket,' I said grimly.

We continued along by the side of the road. I didn't know how far it was to the next town. I had decided that we couldn't risk going to the town where our father used to work, because if anyone were to set out in search of us, that would be one of the most obvious starting places, once they had looked all round our village and the nearby fields. So we had set off in the opposite direction. I knew that we had to reach a station sooner or later, and it didn't matter where we took a train to, provided that it was as far away as possible from our home.

As we trudged along, the light was growing dimmer all the time, but at least it was warm and dry. I tried to pretend that we were setting off on an amazing adventure like two intrepid explorers. I told Sandeep to think about all the places in India and all the places in the world that he would like to visit. I said that I would most want to go to Eden Gardens in Kolkata to watch India play cricket, and the Egyptian Pyramids. Sandeep wanted to watch the cricket as well, and to swim in the sea anywhere and to go to Bollywood, which made me chuckle because there was no such place, but I didn't tell him that. We talked about what animal we would most like to be. Sandeep said a tiger, of course, but I thought I'd really like to be a bird because then I could fly all over the world and land wherever I wanted, which meant I would be able to go to the cricket and the Pyramids. Sandeep growled and said that if he were a tiger he would be able to eat me. He pretended that he was going to pounce, so I started to run. He chased me, laughing wildly. Suddenly, I tripped on a tree root and staggered sideways into a ditch. Sandeep leapt in on top of me. We lay there, puffed out and giggling, until both of us fell silent.

'You said you'd find us some supper,' my brother said at last.

'We had the jack fruit.'

'That wasn't supper. A jack fruit's not supper. I want something else.'

'I can't get anything now, it's too dark to go any further.'

'Where are we going to sleep then?'

'It's quite comfortable here,' I ventured.

Sandeep went quiet again, then mumbled. 'I don't want to sleep in a ditch. There might be rats in it.'

That made me shiver, but I tried to keep my voice calm. 'It's only for tonight, and I'll stay awake.'

'Do you promise?'

'I promise,' I said.

'Amma will be missing us now.' Sandeep sounded tearful. 'I miss Amma.'

'I miss her too.' I squeezed his shoulder. 'We'll write to her as soon as we get a chance.'

'And to Appa?'

'Maybe. But definitely to Amma.'

'What will we tell her?'

'We'll tell her that we're safe and well and that she's not to worry.'

Chapter 7

The best thing about our island was that it had a big patch of grass on it and a low metal fence all round it. The grass made it softer to sleep on. The fence made us feel a bit protected. It was as if it separated us from everything else, especially from the stray dogs and cows that wandered up and down the pavements chewing at anything they could find. They kept away from our island most of the time because they didn't like all the taxis and bicycles and buses and rickshaws that zig-zagged and swerved along the roads surrounding us.

We were shell-shocked from the distress of leaving home and our two days on the run. Our night in the ditch had filled me with anxiety, but I was determined not to let Sandeep know how frightened I was by what we had undertaken. I had scarcely been able to close my eyes for fear that we would be discovered, and I jumped at every slight sound. There were plenty of those as the undergrowth became alive with night-prowling wildlife. Sandeep slept soundly, his head on my chest, his knees digging into the sides of my legs, though in the morning he maintained that he had hardly slept at all.

As soon as it was light enough, I woke him and we set off again. We crept through a village where men were still asleep on the verandahs outside their houses. We hesitated in front of a temple where the priest looked at us searchingly before disappearing behind the statue of Shiva. We skirted round the edge of a coconut plantation and stopped to watch as a man shinned up one of the palms. A woman was sitting by a pile of coconuts that had already been felled. She must have seen the hunger in our stare because she sheared the tops off two of them and held them out for us. We drank the warm juice and when we had finished she cut them in half so that we could attack the flesh.

'No school today?' she asked.

'We don't go to school any more,' I replied.

Sandeep looked up at me in amazement, as though he hadn't thought about this as a consequence of our running away from home.

'That's a shame,' the woman remarked. 'Are you going far?'

'Not too far,' I said cautiously. 'Just to work on my uncle's plantation a little further along.'

'I know most of the people around here,' she said. 'I haven't seen you two before.'

Sandeep took hold of my arm.

'I expect I'll see you when you're on your way home again,' the woman smiled. 'We'll be like old friends then.'

I nodded.

'We could have another coconut,' Sandeep said boldly.

'It's a promise,' said the woman.

I pushed my brother in the back to move him on. We waved goodbye and continued along the track that ran parallel to the road and was screened by overhanging trees. We picked at the coconuts as we walked, and I began to feel that we would be all right if we could just make it to the next town. We hid in the shadows, though, every time a truck or a bus went past, just in case someone was looking for us.

It was another two hours before we reached what seemed to be a junction in the road. As we drew closer

I suddenly realised that it wasn't a junction at all, but a crossing where a railway line ran over the road. Not only that but I could hear a train coming. I had some wild idea that we might be able to flag it down and jump on. We ran as fast as we could to the crossing and waited. Within minutes a blue train hurtled past us, throwing dust into our eyes and deafening us with its horn. We watched it until it had vanished round a corner, then I began to walk quickly after it. 'Come on,' I said to Sandeep. 'If we follow the track we're bound to reach a station eventually.' My brother followed reluctantly behind me, complaining that his feet hurt and that he was hungry again. Not until I said that if we didn't hurry we might have to spend another night in a ditch, did he make any effort to catch up with me.

'Where are we going to sleep when we get to a big town?' he asked.

'Somewhere better than a ditch,' I said.

'What will we do when we get there?'

'I'll find a job so that we'll have money to buy food.' I made myself sound as positive as I could. I couldn't afford to have doubts, not now.

'What will I do?'

'We'll find you a job as well, if you like, and then

when we've got enough money to live on you'll be able to go to school again.'

'What if I don't want to go to school?'

'You'll have to if I say so,' I said firmly. 'School's important, you know that.'

'I don't want to go to a school where I won't know anyone,' Sandeep said sulkily.

'Let's not worry about that now,' I replied. 'Let's just worry about one thing at a time.'

I didn't like all the questions. It was difficult enough for me to hang on to my own belief that we would be all right, without having to deal with Sandeep's doubts as well. I quickened my pace so that it would be too difficult to continue a conversation, and was rewarded when at last I saw opening up ahead of us the distinctive signs of a small town. The railway line veered off behind a filling station and a row of shops, some of which were only just beginning to spill their goods out on to the ground in front of them. We followed the shops round. A man was frying pudlas at one stall and was encircled by men enjoying a late breakfast. The smell snaked deliciously towards us and we hovered in the hope that someone might offer us one. Nobody paid us any attention; after all we still looked well fed and well dressed. We carried on our way, and I knew that we would have to get used to being hungry.

We passed by a temple and another row of shops, then at last found what we were seeking. Several taxis and rickshaws were parked outside a long, white building whose entrance was crammed with people passing through in both directions. This was it. This was the doorway to a new life. I felt my heart leap with excitement and fear. We were so close to being able to make our escape, but we were so close to leaving behind everything we had ever known. I took hold of Sandeep's hand and squeezed it tight.

'Come on,' I said. 'Let's go.'

Chapter 8

It was late at night when we first moved on to the island. I'd thought about going there sooner, but I was scared the police might arrest us and wondered if that was why nobody lived there already. Perhaps the police wouldn't allow it. I was certain that somebody would turn up as soon as it had been dark for a while and tell us that we were trespassing on their land. We watched from a corner opposite, sitting in the rubble of a partially demolished building, hidden by the shadow of a door that was hanging off its hinges. Sandeep was already fed up with waiting. He wanted to know why we couldn't just risk it, he was so desperate to sleep.

I was exhausted too. The train journey from the small town had been long and nerve-wracking. We had managed to slip past the ticket inspector as he dealt with a big family group. We nipped on to the platform and stood by a drinks vendor until a train came in. As soon as one arrived we jumped on board without having any idea of where it was going. The train was crowded and stiflingly hot. There was nowhere to sit and no room to move. Sandeep and I were squashed up against each other in the gap between two carriages, which swivelled and jolted alarmingly over the uneven track. It was only after we had stopped at six different stations that instead of more people pushing on, a larger number jumped off. At each stop I had thought that perhaps we should get off too before we were discovered, but I kept telling myself that if we could just put a little more distance between ourselves and our home it would be better for us.

We finally managed to find seats and began to enjoy watching the changing landscape through the windows. We passed by rice fields where women were bent double pulling up weeds. We passed by villages where bricks were laid out in the sun to dry. We passed by hillsides that were covered in tea bushes. We had both closed our eyes and were beginning to fall asleep when the ticket collector arrived and demanded to see our tickets. When he discovered that not only did we not have tickets but that we had no money to pay for any, he marched us to his cabin at the rear of the train and asked for our name and address so that he could send our parents a bill. I told him that we didn't have any parents and that we lived rough, but he didn't believe us. He threw us off at the next station, with a warning that we would be in serious trouble if we tried to travel again without a ticket.

We pushed our way out of the station to be hit by the barrage of sounds from hundreds of passing vehicles. We just stood and gawped, and wondered how we would ever cross a road if we needed to. What was even worse were the smells. We had been tortured on the train by the men who walked up and down selling vegetable biriani and pakoras and garam chai. A man offered us the remains of a chicken curry he had brought with him, but I was too shy to accept it even though Sandeep dug me with his elbow to say yes. Now, as we gazed along the streets of this strange, daunting city, we were assaulted from all sides by the scents and sights of curry and spices, sweetmeats and pastries, mangoes and pomegranates. There were other smells as well, not so agreeable, from the gaping drains that edged the pavements and into which the city's rubbish spilled.

It was early in the afternoon by then. We spent the rest of the day getting used to the continuous roar of trucks, the blast of horns, the ringing of bells, the shouts of street hawkers and the barking of dogs. We walked up and down one street after another, trying to make sense of the whirl of activity that each one offered up. Our village had one shop and one small temple, a meeting place and forty-five houses. This city had so many shops that I wondered how there could possibly be enough people to buy things from them, even though there were throngs of men and women passing backwards and forwards. Groups were gathered round stalls selling coffee and chai, others were chatting in the entrance to the biggest temple I had ever seen, still more were waiting at bus stops for one of the packed yellow buses that rumbled by. Rickshaw and taxi drivers were parked along the roadside gossiping while they touted for customers. Cyclists wove their way in and out of the other traffic, while rows of abandoned bicycles lined the pavements outside factories and larger stores where their owners had gone to work. We had never seen anything on this scale. We had never seen such tall buildings as we discovered in what we guessed must be the main street. We had never seen a shop that sold everything from balti pans to mobile telephones, from dhotis to western clothes, from medicines to garam masala. One shop had four storeys and all it sold was saris!

'Just think if Amma were here,' I said to Sandeep. 'She would never come out again!'

'How can there be enough saris in the world to fill four floors?' gasped Sandeep.

We didn't dare to go inside any of these large stores in case somebody told us off. We peered through the windows, though, and wondered how much money you would need to have in order to afford all the things that lined the shelves.

'You'd need to be a million, billion, trillionaire,' said Sandeep, shaking his head with wonder.

It made me hopeful that I would be able to get a job if people had so much money, but I was worried too when I saw the number of men, women and children who were begging. Appa had always been adamant that beggars were people who couldn't be bothered to work. He said that they chose not to have a job because it was easier to beg for money. No one in our village begged. If anyone hit hard times, like when my friend Dipak Jangra's father was knocked off his motorcycle and couldn't work for six months, the rest of the villagers got together to help the family. Now, when a woman with a small baby came up to me and

71

held out her hand, I felt terrible because I couldn't give her anything. I tried to hold on to Appa's words, but the woman looked so desperate and I wondered why her family and friends didn't help her. And then I remembered that when Appa had lost his job, he and Amma had both said that there were too many people looking for work and not enough jobs to go round.

What if I couldn't get a job? What would Sandeep and I do then? We didn't have any friends and we didn't have a family any more. We had no money, and only the clothes we were wearing. We still hadn't eaten apart from the coconut early that morning. What if I had no choice other than to beg? I didn't think I could do it. I didn't think I could go to somebody with my hand outstretched and hope that they would take pity on me. I was sure I would prefer to starve. But I knew that I couldn't allow Sandeep to starve, even if in the end it meant that I had to walk every street of the city with my hand outstretched.

My optimism changed quickly to pessimism, which deepened still further when we turned down back streets and saw the cramped housing conditions of so many of the people there. Some of them lived in shacks with the roofs hanging off. Some of them had only a hole in the wall for a window. The houses were all so close to each other that their occupants must have been able to hear their neighbours snoring in the night. At least in our village all the houses had land around them, even if some of them weren't much more than huts. And at least they were clean. Here, there was rubbish blowing around and piles of rubble and other junk on the concrete strips outside the houses. Sandeep kept nudging me to point out children with rags for clothes and no shoes on their feet, who gazed at us through empty eyes from cracked and broken door-steps.

I had such doubts that I had done the right thing. I wanted so much to run back to my mother for guidance. How could I ever have believed that we could survive on our own? I should have thought things through more, taken my time to come to a decision, not run away just because I got hurt. And then I remembered that Amma had been hurt, and hurt too often because of Sandeep and me. I made myself believe again that I had had no choice.

It was only when the shops began to shut as the evening light closed in that we at last had something to eat. We had wandered back to the centre of the city, where I judged it would be safer to sleep. A man who had a stall where he fried puris all day long offered us three that were left over. They were burnt round the edges and had gone hard, but we fell on them greedily as though they were a feast fit for the gods. The man stared at us curiously.

'Hungry, eh?' he said. 'Doesn't your mother feed you?'

Sandeep and I looked at each other but didn't speak.

'I haven't seen you around here before.'

I bit my lip and tried to avoid the man's eyes.

'Ah well,' he said. 'It's none of my business, but I should go back home quickly and get some food inside you if I were you.'

We thanked him for the puris and hurried away before he could ask more questions. I was anxious now to solve the problem of where to sleep. In my mind I had thought that we might find some sort of abandoned building where we would have a roof over our heads to protect us from the sun and rain. I wanted it to be somewhere that would be a proper shelter so that we would be hidden from prying eyes. As we wandered around I quickly realised that there was no such place, not for us at least. Wherever there was a roof, there was someone underneath it. Wherever there were covered doorways, as soon as we hovered close by we became aware that we were being watched.

And so we ended up on the heap of rubble opposite our island, waiting for the darkness to be complete and for all the other street dwellers to take up their positions for the night.

Chapter 9

It was such a relief when we finally moved on to the island, especially when no one challenged us. For what seemed like hours we had watched other street dwellers – men, women and children – settling down for the night on bamboo mats wrapped in ragged blankets under makeshift canopies. We had waited while the traffic died right down, until all that passed by was the occasional taxi or rickshaw. Then we ran quickly across the road, stepped over the little wire fence and stood looking around.

'This is cool,' I grinned at Sandeep. 'We've got our own island.'

'What if someone wants to take it from us?' Sandeep asked.

'We'll tell them we were here first.'

'What if it rains?'

'We'll find some plastic to put over ourselves,' I said brightly, 'but it won't rain tonight.'

We sat down and continued to look around, still expecting that someone would notice us and ask what we thought we were doing.

'Will we stay here for ever?' Sandeep yawned. He lay back on the ground.

'Of course not,' I replied. 'Just until I've found a job.'

'Will we have a proper house then?'

'One day we will.'

Sandeep went quiet and I thought he had gone to sleep. I sat gazing into the night for a while longer. My mind was too full to close it down. I felt as though someone had plucked me from a warm and cosy nest and dropped me into a totally alien landscape, although I knew deep down that the nest had been far from warm and cosy for quite a long time. I had to build a new nest, on my own, and I wanted to make it feel like the safest place on earth. Our island was just a beginning, but I was determined that we would keep it until I could find somewhere even better. I lay down at last and allowed the waves of exhaustion to envelop me.

I was drifting off to sleep when Sandeep's voice broke through the calm.

'I'm scared,' he murmured. 'I don't like the noises.'

I pulled him close. 'Don't be scared,' I said. 'I'll look after you.'

'You told that fortune teller you didn't want to look after me because I'm a pest.'

'That was when you were still seven. You're nine now.'

'Will we go home for my next birthday?' he asked, sitting up suddenly.

'If not, we'll have a big celebration here.' I tried to sound cheerful.

'On our island?'

'In our city,' I whispered through the dark.

Sandeep lay back down and we both fell silent.

We must have fallen asleep, because the next thing I knew I was startled by the blast of a horn very close to my head. I sat up quickly, but it took a few moments for me to work out where I was. It was barely light. I could see a bus disappearing down the road to the left of the island. A truck went by too, circling round us before heading off to the right. My mouth felt like it did when I had a sore throat and cold, and my neck was stiff. I stood up and stretched, working my neck from side to side to loosen it up. As I did so, I saw that I was being watched. A boy was leaning against a lamp post on the corner opposite and staring at me. I turned away from him and pretended to be busy with the belongings in my bag. When I looked up again he was still staring. I began to feel very uneasy. Then he strolled across the road towards us. He stopped outside the wire fence.

'You've got yourself a good place there,' he said.

I nodded. Sandeep began to stir.

'I wish I'd thought of it myself,' the boy continued.

I didn't know what to say. I had the feeling that the boy, who was older than me, was going to claim our island for himself.

'The police will probably move you on if you try to stay.' He watched for my reaction. 'Some of the police round here are mean, especially to street kids.'

I nodded my head again as Sandeep sat up, rubbing his eyes.

'I should know,' said the boy. 'They beat me up once.'

'The police did?' I said, shocked.

'They threw me in a cell and beat me up.'

'Why?' I asked.

'Because they could, I suppose,' the boy replied. He shrugged his shoulders. 'Most of them are all right though. It's just one or two who aren't.'

I stood there awkwardly, wondering where the conversation would go next, while Sandeep stared up at the boy, wide-eyed at what he had told us.

'You going to stay around this city, then?' the boy asked.

I nodded for the third time, wishing I could think of something to say to make myself appear tougher. I didn't want this boy to think that I couldn't look after myself and my brother.

'My name's Vikas,' he offered. 'I've got the contacts if you need a job.'

'I'm Suresh and my brother's Sandeep,' I replied. I didn't say anything else. It would have been giving too much away to tell this stranger that I needed to find a job, and I wasn't sure that any job he might propose would be one that I would want to take. After all, his clothes were ragged and dirty, his hair was long, and he didn't have any shoes on his feet. I watched him go back across the road and pick up a large sack from the pavement. He didn't look back but turned off along a side street and was quickly out of sight.

'Did you like that boy?' Sandeep asked.

'He seemed friendly,' I said.

'He smelt,' Sandeep said dismissively.

It was true, but I didn't respond because I was wondering where and when we would be able to wash ourselves. There hadn't been an opportunity since we had left home.

It was growing steadily lighter and the traffic was increasing. I saw the looks of amusement on the faces of the rickshaw-wallahs as they drove round our island, and decided that it was time to move off it for the day before the police noticed us. We packed our bags and crossed the road, hoping that we might soon find something to eat. Some street dwellers were still wrapped in their blankets, asleep in doorways. Others were sitting and staring into space, though they gazed at us curiously as we went by. There were few people up and about so early, apart from us and traders whom we discovered were going to market to stock up with items for their shops. We tagged along behind a group of them, because that way we attracted less attention.

When we came to the market, we stopped just inside the entrance and watched with fascination as the street traders and market stallholders haggled vigorously over prices and quantities. There was everything there, from huge sacks of rice to piles of coir mats to tanks of live crabs and lobsters. We had never before seen so many fruits and vegetables and spices and different cuts of meat. The noise and the heat were suffocating, but we couldn't drag ourselves away.

I wondered if one of the stallholders might offer me a job if I asked. There were quite a few younger men helping to pack boxes with purchases the street traders had made. Others were carrying sacks on their heads and taking them to the traders' ox carts or trucks or hired rickshaws, which were parked outside. I didn't have the nerve to ask, though, and in any case it wasn't really the sort of work I wanted to do. I hoped, rather, to find a job as an office boy in one of the big stores we had seen, or with a company that dealt in insurance or finance or some other kind of respectable business. If Ramit Tandon, with all his nervous twitches, could find employment in my father's office, surely I could do the same?

A pile of fruit collapsed from a stall close by us. Sandeep immediately dived upon an apple that rolled towards his feet. He was about to sink his teeth into it, when I saw the stallholder glaring. I took the apple from my brother and bent down to help collect the rest of the fruit. Sandeep hissed angrily at me, but I hissed back that we were not thieves however hungry we might be. He muttered something about my being stupid. I ignored him and continued to help. The owner was so grateful that, when all the fruit was back in place, he gave me a bag of apples and pomegranates for my trouble. As we left the market, Sandeep demanded that I share them with him.

'Only if you promise never to steal,' I insisted.

'I promise,' he said grudgingly. Then he added, 'What if we're dying of starvation?'

'We won't be,' I said.

Chapter 10

That day felt like the longest of my life. We wandered the streets for hour after hour with nothing to do and no particular place to go. The novelty of being somewhere we had never been before quickly wore off as our legs grew tired and our bellies grumbled at the lack of a proper meal. I tried to make myself go inside one of the big stores to ask for work, but I was so daunted by the idea that I kept putting it off, telling myself that I should wait until I had explored every corner of the city before deciding which place would be likely to provide the best opportunity. If I left it until the following day, it would give me more time to think.

Sandeep trailed along beside me, complaining occasionally that he was bored or hungry or tired. Every so often we flopped down by a wall to rest. We watched the townspeople going about their business and wondered where the other street children disappeared to during the day. We saw two boys begging, but apart from that there was no sign of them. When we passed by a school at lunchtime, the children there stared at us through the grilles in the gates and several of them asked us why we weren't in school too. I didn't answer, but Sandeep called out that we had more important things to do. I told him off for that. I didn't want him to start believing that school was unimportant.

By the middle of the afternoon, all the doubts I had ever had that we could manage on our own in this unsympathetic city were pressing heavily down upon me. The dust, the dirt, the noise, the crowded streets, the poverty, the lack of any green fields or open spaces, all combined to drain the confidence I had felt when we had finally caught our train and, then, when we had moved on to our island. Those moments of triumph were tiny compared to the mountain I would have to climb if we were to survive. I had to be braver, I knew that. I had to swallow my fear and go into those big buildings and make them give me a job by telling them that I was the best they could find. Tomorrow. I would do it tomorrow. And until then I would practise in my head what I was going to say to persuade them.

We walked down a street that we hadn't previously explored. A high wooden fence lined one side of it, but a little way along there was a gap. We could hear voices as we drew closer and a noise like something being hit with a hammer. We reached the gap and looked through. There was a huge area of barren ground where a building had been demolished. On it a group of boys were playing cricket. One of them spotted us straight away and beckoned to us to join them. Sandeep was through the fence like a rocket, while I hesitated because I would rather have found something out about them first. And then I saw that the boy who was batting was Vikas. We needed friends, I told myself. We needed a break from tramping the streets. I scrambled through the gap and took up a place in the field next to Sandeep. The boy who was bowling ran in and Vikas gave the ball an almighty wallop in my direction. I tried to stop it but it bounced on the bumpy ground, jumped over my hands and ran all the way to the fence.

'Hey, the new kid's got butter fingers,' the bowler sniggered.

'He's the islander I told you about. He's found himself a better place to live than you have,' Vikas grinned.

86

'And I've got me a better pair of hands than he has,' the boy called back. 'What's your name, islander?'

'Suresh,' I said, flushing with embarrassment.

'And I'm Sandeep,' my brother piped up.

'That's Arun you're talking to,' Vikas informed us. 'Watch out he doesn't steal your island from you when you're not looking. He'd steal his grandmother's false teeth if he could find a use for them.'

All the boys fell about laughing, while Arun adopted a hurt expression. 'That's not a nice thing to say about someone who merely tries to redistribute wealth from time to time.'

'You can use fancy words all you like,' chuckled Vikas, 'but it still amounts to the same thing. Now get on and bowl, will you, before it gets dark.'

'Big fat bouncer coming up, then,' warned Arun. 'You better be ready to duck.' He strode back up the pitch. Vikas bent over his makeshift bat.

'Ready and waiting,' he chanted.

Arun paddled his foot like a bull about to rampage, then charged down the pitch and hurled the ball towards the wicket. Vikas swung his bat and hit the ball as hard as he could. It flew high in the air, up and up. It was mine to catch. I ran as fast as I could. It started to come down and for a moment I lost it in the sun. And then I caught sight of it again, held out my hands as I dived, and felt the round roughness when I pulled it in to my chest. There were cheers from the boys and Sandeep galloped over to me to share my triumph. I sat up to see Vikas throw down the bat.

'I knew we shouldn't have let you play,' he said grimly. He marched across the ground towards me. I shrank backwards, but when he reached me he pulled me to my feet.

'Now listen and listen hard,' he hissed into my face. 'If you want to survive around here, then you obey the rules, and the rules are that when your olders and betters are batting you don't catch them out. Got it? Have you got it?'

I nodded quickly and apologised.

He glared at me for a moment longer then broke into laughter and cuffed me playfully across the top of the head. 'You've got a lot to learn, kiddo. Don't ever let yourself be bullied like that or you won't last two seconds in this city.' He went to walk away, then turned back. 'That was a great catch,' he said. 'We'll have you in our team.'

I thought for a second, then said carefully, 'If I play, my brother plays.'

It was Arun who laughed this time. 'Hey, that islander's a fast learner. He's telling *us* what to do now.'

'As long as your brother earns his place,' Vikas agreed. 'Now can you stop holding things up and let us get on with the game? It'll be too dark soon.'

We took up our positions again while another boy went in to bat. As the afternoon went by, I felt as if a great weight was being lifted from my shoulders, because I no longer felt alone. This group of boys accepted us without needing to know anything more about us other than that, like them, we were living on the streets. Meeting them helped us through that first day. The hours of walking aimlessly around were broken by an hour of fun and laughter. When it came to an end, when the light was too bad, I half expected that we would all go off somewhere to spend the evening together. I waited for some indication that we were to be invited to join the others, but one by one they drifted away on their own, until Sandeep and I were left hovering by the fence, the cricket pitch behind now reduced to a desolate wasteland.

We went back to wandering the streets. Some of the shops were beginning to close. We tried to find the road where we had been offered leftover puris the evening before. By the time we reached the spot where the stallholder had his oven, we were too late. The shutters were already across it, a sweet smell lingering in the air to remind us of what we were missing. We kept on going, hesitating in front of every stall that was still serving food, but nobody paid us much attention. Soon the last of the shops closed and we were left to trek back to our island, hungry and despondent. We sat in the rubble of the partially demolished building, waiting for the quiet of the night.

'You promised we wouldn't die of starvation,' Sandeep reproached me.

'We won't,' I replied firmly.

'But I'm dying of starvation now.'

'You're hungry, that's all.'

'I'm more than hungry. I feel like I'm going to pass out.'

'You won't pass out, and as soon as we get on to our island you can go to sleep.'

'I'm too hungry to sleep.' Sandeep was sounding more and more irritable. 'You said you'd get a job and then we'd have money to buy food.'

'I will get a job,' I insisted. 'I'll get a job tomorrow.'

'What if you don't? We'll be even more starving then.'

I couldn't stop the tide of questions, accusations, demands. I was hungry too, but I knew that it was something we were going to have to get used to, along with being dirty and frightened and tired and uncomfortable.

'Why can't we just go and ask someone for something to eat?' Sandeep continued.

'Beg, you mean?' I said coldly.

'No, not beg. Just ask.'

'It's the same thing.'

'Not if we ask nicely. Not if we say please and don't pester.'

'I'm not doing that, and neither are you. Come on, let's go over to our island.'

'You can't stop me,' said Sandeep. 'You can't tell me what to do all the time.'

I stood up and began to cross the road. Sandeep didn't move. I kept on going, certain that he would follow. When I reached the island and looked round I couldn't see him.

'Sandeep,' I called out. 'Sandeep, stop playing games.' I tore back across the road. He had gone from the rubble. 'Sandeep!' I yelled. There was no reply. He was nowhere to be seen. I couldn't believe he could be so foolish as to run off. He could get lost in the dark and spend the night trying to find his way back. He could run into the police, who would want to know where he was from and what he was doing. Other possibilities sprang into my mind. I pushed them angrily away. 'Sandeep!' I yelled again. There were too many streets going in too many directions for me to consider searching for him. I crossed back over to the island and stood there gazing out like a shipwrecked sailor.

A movement to my left made me spin round.

'Where's that brother of yours?' a voice said.

It was Arun. My heart sank for a moment because I thought that he might want to cause me trouble, especially now that I was on my own.

'He'll be back in a minute,' I said.

'He's a bit young to be wandering around on his own at night,' Arun observed.

I shrugged my shoulders.

'That Vikas is right about this island. I wouldn't mind it for myself.'

I glared at him, waiting for him to challenge me for it. He grinned at me broadly. 'Fancy a new kid fetching himself the best place in town,' he said. 'Well, islander, I reckon you've shown us all up big time. Mind you, it won't be so great when it rains.'

He was about to go away when I heard the sound of footsteps approaching.

'Suresh, are you all right?' Sandeep's voice was cautious.

'Well, well, well, it's little brother,' chuckled Arun. 'And what have you got there, little brother?'

'Just something to eat.' Sandeep stepped on to the island and stood behind me.

'And there's me with my belly as empty as the temple at midnight,' said Arun.

'It's not for you,' Sandeep replied hotly.

'Where did you get it?' I asked, wishing that Arun would leave us alone.

'A man gave it to me.'

I knew straight away that Sandeep was lying.

'A man gave it to you!' whistled Arun. 'Well, I wish you would just show me that man so that he can give me some too.'

'He's gone,' Sandeep said quickly, 'and there wasn't any more left.'

'Well, that's a big shame, little brother. I guess I'll have to eat the soles of my shoes tonight, I'm so hungry. Remember me as you tuck into your feast.' Arun laughed loudly and loped off down the road.

'I don't like him very much,' muttered Sandeep.

It wasn't Arun I was concerned about at that moment. I turned angrily on my brother. 'Don't you ever run off like that again,' I fumed. 'You had me worried sick.'

'No need to be,' said Sandeep. 'I didn't go far and I'm not a baby.'

'Where did you get that food from?'

'I found it. Outside a restaurant. There was a dog trying to get it, but I got it first.' He sounded almost triumphant.

'And you think it'll be all right to eat?' I said incredulously.

'It's better than nothing, and it tastes fine,' he retorted, pulling open the plastic bag he was holding. Inside were two pieces of chicken wrapped up in half a piece of nan bread. They were covered in ash, which Sandeep brushed away before raising one of the pieces to his mouth.

'Don't,' I said sharply. 'It could make you ill.'

He ignored me and bit into it. I grabbed it from his hand and threw it into the road, then hurled the other piece after it. 'If you get food poisoning you could die,' I hissed.

'If I starve I could die,' he hissed back. He was about to run into the road to pick the pieces up when a truck rumbled by. Its wheels rolled right over them. Sandeep was furious. He punched me hard on the arm, but I couldn't help laughing. The sight of the squashed chicken thighs was just too much. At first he thought I was laughing at him, which made him even more angry, but then he too saw the funny side and began to giggle.

We sat down at last, exhausted. Sandeep grabbed at the piece of nan bread, which I had accidentally trodden on, and bit into it. 'You can't stop me having this,' he challenged. 'This won't make me ill.'

I hoped it wouldn't. I watched him stuff it into his mouth as fast as possible in case I tried to take it from him. I felt a large pang of guilt that I had reduced him to scavenging and eating like a ravenous wild animal. Amma would have been horrified if she could have seen him. I wondered how long it would be, how hungry I would have to be, to stop caring too.

Exhausted though I was, it took me ages to get to sleep that night. In my mind I kept playing over and over again the events of the day. The cricket game had been such fun after the hours of trudging round the streets. I hoped we would be allowed to play again and make some friends. Vikas seemed to be the one all the other boys respected, and he seemed to think he could get me a job. If I couldn't find anything else, and I would start searching properly in the morning, then I would ask him what sort of job he could offer. I wasn't so sure about Arun, though. Hadn't he admitted that he thought stealing was all right? I decided that he couldn't be trusted and that I would keep out of his way as much as possible.

Chapter 11

I didn't find a job the next day. Since we had left home the days had become a blur, and I hadn't realised that it was a Sunday. I woke up later than usual, partly, I think, because I was growing used to the noise, but also because that morning it was strangely quiet. I rolled over and stretched, then sat up and immediately felt dizzy. The sun was already quite high in the sky, and it was hot and humid. My shirt was sticking to my back and my throat was parched. I turned to wake Sandeep. To my horror I saw that he wasn't there. I stood up, rocky on my feet, and cursed him for disappearing again. Then I heard laughter. I tried to focus my eyes through the glare of the sun and the dust and my own light-headedness. I almost tripped over the fence. A taxi drove past, its driver blowing his horn at me and waving his arms. I had stepped into the road without noticing.

'Suresh, what's wrong, Suresh?' I heard someone calling as I struggled to get my bearings.

I tried to answer but nothing came out. I felt I was losing my balance until something caught my arms and steadied me.

'I'll get him something to drink,' someone said.

There was a sound of feet running. I closed my eyes and collapsed on to my knees.

'Don't die, Suresh.' My brother's frightened voice was close to my ear. 'I won't know what to do if you die.'

Why did he think I was going to die? I lifted my arm and tried to find his hand. He slipped it into mine and I squeezed it. 'Just a bit hot,' I managed to say.

'Arun's gone to get you a drink.'

For a moment I couldn't think who Arun was, then I wondered where he was going to get me a drink from.

'He got me some breakfast. Bananas and hot rogani roti. He'll get you some as well if I ask him to. We didn't want to wake you up before, but I woke up really early and Arun was sitting on the corner and he waved at me so I went over to talk to him. Even though I didn't like him before, I do now and he says he can help us so we don't have to starve.'

I listened to the rush of words, a knot of anxiety forming in my stomach. I didn't want Sandeep being influenced by a stranger, especially one who, by his own admission, 'redistributed wealth'. The trouble was that until I could offer my brother something better, I knew that he was easy prey for someone like Arun, though I wondered why Arun would want to bother with him.

'Bottle of fizzy orange for the invalid,' I heard.

A shadow fell across me.

'Lift his head up, little brother.'

I wished I could resist. I wished I could take back control, but I was too weak and in any case my body craved the sweet drink I was being offered. I pulled it to my lips and guzzled so greedily that some of it spilled down my chin and my neck.

'That's a big thirst you've got on you, islander,' snickered Arun. 'Didn't your mother tell you that only camels can go without water, and even they can't go without for ever?'

'Amma did tell us that, of course she did,' said Sandeep seriously.

I sat up slowly, feeling a lot better already, though my head was thumping.

'Looks to me like you should go back to your mother,' Arun continued.

'Why should we?' I muttered.

'You may have found yourselves a nice little island, but you're not savvy enough to live on the streets, that's why,' he said bluntly.

'We've only just got here.'

'And you need someone to wipe your bottom already.'

'We're doing all right,' I argued. I stood up to try and put some distance between myself and this boy who was trying to make me look stupid. 'Today I'm going to get a job and then we'll be fine.'

Arun hooted with laughter. 'What sort of job are you going to find yourself on a Sunday, eh? Most places are closed.'

I hadn't even thought of it. No wonder the streets were so quiet. 'Tomorrow, then,' I said.

'They don't give jobs to street kids,' Arun grimaced. 'They want to know that you come from a nice cosy home with nice respectable parents.'

'We do,' I said. 'Or did.'

'And what are you going to put for an address? The island?'

'I'll make one up.'

'Do you think we haven't all tried that?' Arun laughed again. 'They soon find you out.'

'Why don't you just leave us alone?' I stormed.

'That's friendly, when I've just fetched you a life-saving bottle of fizz.' He held up his hands as though fending off an attack. 'I was just about to offer you some food as well.'

The thought of food made my stomach leap, but I told him that I didn't need his food and that I could get my own.

Sandeep butted in. 'Arun's being nice to you,' he said crossly, 'so why are you being horrible to him?'

'Because we've got this far on our own and I don't need him to tell me what to do.' I watched Sandeep exchange glances with Arun. I knew I was being stubborn and unreasonable, but I didn't trust Arun's motives and I didn't want him making me look small in front of my brother.

'I'll leave you to it, then,' Arun said breezily. He sauntered off across the road.

'You've upset him now,' Sandeep said accusingly once Arun was out of sight.

'He upset me too,' I muttered. I was too tired and weak to cope with an argument. I needed Sandeep to be on my side and support me, just as I would support him. I hated the thought of other people causing divisions between us. 'Come on,' I said, trying to sound more cheerful, 'let's go and explore round the outside of the city.'

We set off in silence. Sandeep trudged along, scuffing his shoes on the ground to let me know that he was still cross with me. I wanted to tell him not to do it, because once that pair of shoes was worn out he might not have another, but I dared not upset him and anyway I was fed up with the role of parent. I began to miss Amma more and more as we watched families spilling out on to the streets, the women's Sunday saris shining brightly, the children happy that the gates of their schools were firmly shut. Many of the shops were closed, but there were hawkers everywhere selling flower garlands and trinkets and colourful statues of the gods. The smell of sweet pastries wafted through the air from the roadside griddles, and hot steam spread from the stalls serving coffee and chai. Groups of people stood around chattering and drinking, while others strode purposefully along on their way to visit friends and relatives. A crowd was gathered outside the cinema waiting for its doors to open. We hovered nearby, taking in the huge, glitzy pictures which showed a world even more different than ever from our own. Meanwhile, along the sides of every road, taxi drivers and rickshaw-wallahs competed with each other to attract customers who wanted to spend the day away from the city. I wished we had the money to hire one ourselves, my feet ached so much. It made me still more determined that somehow or other I would earn enough to feed myself and my brother, to go to the cinema one day and to hire a rickshaw whenever we needed to.

We turned down a road that led away from the centre of the city. There were fewer shops now, and none that were open, apart from the occasional general store where the owners sat on chairs outside hoping that someone would go in. They looked up and greeted us, but quickly lost interest when they saw we were going to walk past. I had no real idea where we were headed, but I hoped that we might come to a river or fields or open spaces. Somewhere peaceful and free from the noise and frenzy of the city. As we continued down one side street after another, the houses became shabbier but the people who lived there had decorated their doorsteps with signs of welcome. Children waved at us, then giggled and ran indoors, while their mothers stared at us curiously. I felt much more at home there, but I was also aware that we were attracting a lot of attention. One boy ran out and asked us our names and where we were going.

Another asked us where we lived and why he hadn't seen us before. I became anxious to get back to the city centre where nobody took any notice of us.

At last we came to the end of the maze of small streets and found ourselves entering a huge wasteland. It was skirted on one side by a railway track and on the other by a ramshackle mess of bricks, plastic sheeting, corrugated iron, scorched palm branches and mud, which stretched for as far as we could see. Children were running around on the stony ground, barefoot and raggedly dressed. Women carrying large, coloured metal pitchers were queuing by a standpipe to fill them with water. Others were laying clothes out to dry on stray bushes and rocks. Old men squatted on piles of rubble chewing paan and gazing into space.

I thought we must have stumbled upon the city slums. Appa had been fond of warning us that if we didn't do our schoolwork, if we didn't find a good job, then that was where we might finish up. He said it jokingly, but Appa's jokes often had an edge to them.

'I don't like it here,' Sandeep said. 'Let's go back.'

I hesitated. I had been watching a young boy and girl who were running across the wasteground in the direction of the railway track. I hadn't noticed before, but rising up behind the track was an enormous rubbish tip that spread for some distance. I could see men, women and children dotted about on it, bent double and sifting through the rubbish. Each time they found something they wanted, they put it in the sacks they were carrying. When the young boy and girl reached the track, they pushed their way through the scatter of bushes that bordered it, darted across and disappeared for a few seconds behind the undergrowth on the other side. They reappeared halfway up the tip and began ferreting around like everyone else.

'What are they doing?' Sandeep asked.

'Collecting things,' I said.

'But it's all rubbish,' he scoffed.

A train came hurtling through at that moment and stole my brother's next words. I was about to turn away and head back to the city when I heard someone calling us.

'Hey, islanders, wait for me.'

I saw a hand waving and then, when the bushes parted, Vikas. He had a sack over his shoulder and a broad grin on his face.

'I didn't expect to see posh islanders in a place like this,' he said.

I was so shocked I couldn't answer.

'I've got some rich pickings today,' he continued.

'Come on, let's go and find somewhere to sit and I'll share them with you.'

'Did you get them from the dump?' Sandeep asked incredulously.

'One man's dump is another man's gold mine,' laughed Vikas. 'You wait and see.'

I was too intrigued to say no. We followed Vikas as he swaggered across the wasteground and found a rock a distance away from the slum dwellers. We sat down with him and waited while he delved into his sack.

'Who wants a drink?' he said, pulling out a large bottle of Coke.

'Me!' said Sandeep immediately.

'What's wrong with it?' I wanted to know.

'Bit out of date, that's all,' Vikas replied. 'Only a bit, and it doesn't go off, well, not straight away.'

He opened the bottle. There wasn't much of a hiss as he did so, but I no longer cared about the wisdom of drinking it, and I didn't want to feel like I had that morning. Vikas took a quick swig, said it tasted fine and handed it to me. I had a sip, then drank so long and hard that Sandeep and Vikas both yelled in protest.

'Good, eh?' Vikas said when all three of us had had some and were belching loudly.

'What's next?' piped up Sandeep.

'Next we've got ourselves a tiffin box with some vegetable biriani, half a chapatti and some dal tarka,' Vikas said proudly.

'A feast,' I grinned. At the same time I remembered what I had said to Sandeep only the night before about scavenging. When Vikas produced a tiffin box that was cracked and broken on one side, I warned Sandeep that it wasn't safe to eat it.

'If Vikas eats it then I'm going to eat it,' he argued.

'Stay cool, big brother,' Vikas said to me. 'If it doesn't smell right, I won't be eating it. If it smells OK then there's nothing wrong with it. I have a nose for good and bad.'

He picked some out with his fingers, lifted it to his nose, sniffed ceremoniously and smiled. 'This nose says it smells good, so this mouth is going to eat it.' When he had finished and licked his fingers clean, he passed the tiffin box to me. I decided that I had to trust it, I was so hungry. I took a handful and gave the box to Sandeep.

'Lakshmi is smiling on us today,' said Vikas contentedly.

I nodded to show my appreciation of his generosity, but I wondered that he could be so grateful for a meal that somebody else had thrown away.

'Do you live here?' Sandeep asked, a question that had been on the tip of my own tongue.

'No fear,' scoffed Vikas. 'You wouldn't catch me living in this hole. I live in the city centre, like you. I've got my own doorway and a water pump close by. Better than a lot of people.'

I wanted to ask him why he lived on the streets and how long he had been there and what job he did, but I didn't want him to think I was prying. And then Sandeep asked what else he had in his sack.

'Cans,' he said. 'That's what I deal in. Thirty-two I found today. My worst day was eight and my best was fifty-five.' He opened the sack to show us and pulled out a torn pink pashmina at the same time. 'Do you think it suits me?' he grinned, wrapping it round his neck.

'No,' I grinned back. 'It doesn't go with your eyes.'

'I don't care,' he huffed. 'It'll make a good pillow.'

'What do you mean you deal in cans?' asked Sandeep.

I gave him a sharp look because I was worried that we would drive Vikas away with our questions, even if I did want to know the answers myself.

'I recycle them,' Vikas replied, with a touch of what sounded like pride in his voice. 'That's my job. I'm a ragpicker.' He jumped down from the rock. 'It's a good job,' he said. 'You should think about it.'

With that he set off back towards the city, leaving us to wonder at the idea that anyone could think digging through other people's rubbish was a good job. We were grateful, though. Because of his job we had eaten. We wouldn't eat again that day.

Chapter 12

I plucked up the courage to ask for a job the next morning. In the window of a small office building, there was an advertisement for a boy to run errands. It wasn't really what I wanted, but at least I knew that they needed somebody. I told Sandeep to wait outside, then knocked on the door and went in. There was a woman sitting at a desk just inside. She looked me up and down and I instantly wished that I had been able to wash my clothes.

'Can I help you?' she asked.

'I've come about the job,' I said.

'You're too young.'

I stood up straighter. 'I'm sixteen,' I said.

'And I'm your mother,' she countered. She stared at me as if daring me to argue. I didn't argue. I fled, my heart pounding so loudly that I thought Sandeep would be able to hear it.

'They don't want you, do they?' he said.

I shook my head.

'When are we going to eat today?'

The problem of how, where and when we were going to eat nagged away at me from the moment I woke up in the morning until we rediscovered our island at night. I was almost growing used to being hungry; not the sort of hungry we would feel after a day at school, but a gnawing hunger that sat in the pit of our stomachs and seemed slowly to devour us from the inside. Growing used to it and liking it were two different things though, and I could feel myself becoming weaker and more tired, which was also caused by the fact that we could never sleep for long enough. I could see the dark circles under my brother's eyes and how his clothes were already beginning to look loose on him.

'We'll find something soon,' I said, linking arms with him.

We wandered down one of the main streets. Having been so quickly and sharply rebuffed in my first attempt to get a job, I was nervous about trying again. I would have to, though, either that or go home. I stared into a shop window and saw a reflection of myself. I looked like one of the poorer children from our village, one of those who spent their days in the fields. I looked beaten-down already. I wondered how Vikas and Arun managed to walk around with such a swagger, as if they were important people in the community.

There was a commotion behind me. I swung round to see a figure sprinting down the road followed by the owner of a cigarette kiosk. The man pulled up sharply as soon as he realised that his chase was futile and growled, 'Bloody street kids.'

Sandeep nudged me. 'I'm sure that was Arun,' he whispered.

'It wouldn't surprise me,' I muttered. 'Come on, let's go somewhere else.'

'Are you going to get a job today?' he asked.

'I'm trying, aren't I?' I replied irritably.

We passed by a skinny, ragged little boy, not much older than Sandeep, who asked me if he could shine my shoes. I looked down at them and saw how filthy they had become. I gazed at the boy and saw that by comparison with him we must still appear much better off. I shook my head. The boy pleaded with me to say yes and promised that he would do a good job. I said we had no money. He cursed us as we moved away.

'How did he afford his shoe-shine things?' Sandeep wanted to know.

I shrugged my shoulders as it occurred to me that in one way the boy was richer than us. He had a shoe-shine kit with which he could earn his living and we didn't even have that. And he had something to do to pass the time. As well as being penniless and hungry, I was bored with tramping the streets for hours on end. The time spent with Vikas at the dump had provided some relief the day before, and the game of cricket had been brilliant, but every morning opened up with nothing to look forward to.

We came to a small hotel. I determined to try again. 'Stay there while I go in,' I said to Sandeep. I plunged through the doors and strode over to the reception desk. 'Can I see someone about a job?' I asked the man who was standing there.

'You could see me,' he said. 'What sort of job are you looking for?'

'Anything,' I said. 'I could learn to be a waiter. I'm strong. I could be a porter.'

'How old are you?'

'Sixteen,' I said firmly.

The man stared at me but didn't say anything.

'I'll work hard, I promise.' I tried not to sound too desperate, but there was a quiver in my voice.

'You look as if you could do with a good meal,' he said. 'Where are you from?'

I didn't have time to answer before he said, 'You're not from round here, are you?'

'I just moved here.'

'Where are you living?'

I tried to think of one of the street names I had seen. I was too slow. He looked me straight in the eyes. 'We don't employ street dwellers,' he said. 'And you're too young, anyway. Sorry.'

He reached behind him and picked up a bottle of water. I was getting ready to run when he came round to the front of the desk. 'If you go outside, to the back of the building,' he said quietly, 'I've just thrown out some pizzas. Chef cooked too many for a party last night.' He pressed the bottle of water into my hands and ushered me to the door.

'Thank you,' I said awkwardly. 'Thank you very much.'

'Just don't let me catch you sleeping on our steps, that's all,' he replied.

Sandeep couldn't believe it when I told him about the pizzas. He darted off and reappeared with a black plastic sack while I was still trying to gather my thoughts about what had happened.

114

'There's six in here!' he called triumphantly. 'Six whole pizzas!'

'And water.' I forced myself to smile and waved the bottle at him. 'Let's go and find a special place to eat our meal.'

We walked up the road to a deep stretch of pavement backed by a high wall, where we passed a number of craftsmen. In front of each of them, laid out on cloths stretched over the pavement, were pieces they had already finished and were hoping to sell. The men looked poor and nobody seemed to be buying from them. When we reached an empty space, we sat down against the wall. Sandeep got out two of the pizzas. I opened the bottle and guzzled thirstily.

'You've got to share it!' he cried when I stopped for breath.

I handed it over, grabbed one of the pizzas and took a big bite.

I don't think anything had ever tasted so wonderful. If we had been sitting in the very best restaurant in the whole of India, nothing on the menu would have tasted as good. I closed my eyes and chewed contentedly.

'Did you get a job?' Sandeep nudged my arm. 'Did they give you a job?'

It was the question that plunged me back into the black hole of doubt about how we were going to survive. It was the question I didn't want to answer. I tore myself another piece of pizza and bit into it savagely. 'I got us some food, didn't I?' I growled.

Sandeep went silent. He began to pick bits off his pizza, uncrossed his legs then crossed them again. 'What if we could get some shoe-shine stuff?' he said at last.

'What if we could?' I replied. 'There's already a shoe-shine boy on every corner.'

'Perhaps we could do the same as Vikas, just until we find something else,' he suggested.

'Be ragpickers you mean?'

'Just for a while.'

I tore off another piece of pizza, but I didn't feel like eating it any more. However hard I had wanted to believe that we would never finish up picking through someone else's rubbish, I was beginning to realise that we might not have any choice. I may only have tried for two jobs, but it was clear that people weren't fooled by my age. It was clear too that I would struggle to find anything worthwhile, because after less than a week I was already labelled as a street kid. Without a proper address, I didn't think anybody honourable would employ me.

I still wasn't prepared to give in, though. Not just yet. I had to trust that Ganesh would remove some of the obstacles we faced and help us on our way. Amma had always said that the elephant god would provide for us and tell us what to do in times of trouble. 'Think how ashamed Amma would be of us,' I muttered.

Chapter 13

I was woken in the middle of the night by a scuffling sound close to my head. A dog was eating our pizzas. I cried out with anger. I clapped my hands to frighten it away, then tried to grab hold of the sack. The dog growled through gritted teeth and I backed off as Sandeep woke up.

'What's the matter? What's happening?' he croaked. He quickly understood and jumped to his feet. The sudden movement alarmed the dog. It turned and snapped at him, catching him on the leg. He squealed with pain. I picked up my bag and threw it. The dog snarled as it knocked him sideways, but it made off down the road, the bag of pizzas in its mouth.

'It bit me, Suresh,' Sandeep whimpered.

I bent down to look at his leg. It was difficult to see

in the dark, but I could feel the wetness of blood. 'It's not much,' I said, 'but we need to clean it.'

'I won't get rabies, will I?' he whimpered again as I dabbed at the blood with the corner of my shirt.

'You'll be all right. It's only a scratch.'

'Amma always said a scratch is all it takes,' he murmured, then he burst into tears. 'I want to go home now,' he wailed. 'I don't like it here and I want to see Amma. Please let's go home, Suresh.'

I took him in my arms and fought back my own tears. 'We can't go home, you know we can't.' I tried to sound strong. 'I don't even know how to get home from here, and Appa will be even angrier if we go back.'

'Can't we ask Amma to come here?' Sandeep sobbed.

'Amma can't leave Appa. It's her duty to look after him.'

'But who is going to look after us?'

'We can look after ourselves. I can look after you.' I squeezed his shoulder.

'Doesn't Amma love us enough?'

'I didn't want her to have to choose between Appa and us, you know that, Sandeep. It's better this way. Appa will be nicer to Amma now we've gone.' I had to keep believing that or it would all have been a waste of time.

'We've got nothing to eat again,' sniffed Sandeep.

'Something will turn up,' I said. 'It always does.'

We tried to go back to sleep, but we were both too miserable. We lay on our island looking up at the stars and talking about days in our childhood when life had seemed so easy. We remembered walks by the river and watching the otters at play. We remembered sitting under the neem tree, being bombarded with fruit skins by monkeys. There were no monkeys in this city. Cattle, goats, pigs, hens, dogs, but no monkeys. The last days we remembered being happy were when we had played cricket with Appa and all the other village boys, and when we had gone to the river with Amma, where the funny little old man had made his parrot tell our fortunes.

'He told me I was going to be a leader,' said Sandeep.

'He told me I would look after you, which makes me the leader,' I countered.

'Only for the moment,' said Sandeep.

'While you're still a baby,' I chuckled.

He leapt on top of me and pummelled me with his fists. I caught hold of his wrists so that he ended up hitting the air. 'You're not strong enough,' I laughed. He started to bounce up and down on my stomach. 'All right, all right, I give in,' I puffed. He fell off sideways and we both lay there panting until I became aware that a car had pulled up across the road from us. I sat up quickly. It was a police car. A policeman was striding towards us.

'What's going on here?' he asked when he reached the island.

'Nothing, sir,' I replied.

'Were you fighting?'

'No, sir.'

'Why aren't you at home in bed?'

I couldn't answer, but Sandeep piped up, 'We haven't got a home, sir.'

'Street kids, eh? I ought to have you locked up for brawling.'

'Please don't, sir,' I begged. 'We won't cause any trouble.'

'Is this where you're sleeping?'

I looked at Sandeep and back to the policeman. 'Yes, sir,' I said, 'but we're not doing any harm.'

I thought I saw a faint smile on his lips. 'I'll give you ten out of ten for invention, that's for sure,' he said.

'It's the best place we could find, sir.'

'How are you earning money to live?'

'I'm looking for a job, sir.'

'You'd better make sure you find one. We don't want any more people begging on our streets. And don't think that just because I've let you get away with it this time, one of my colleagues won't come along and put you inside if they catch you causing a rumpus in the middle of the night.'

'We're very grateful to you, sir,' I said as he began to walk off.

He turned back to us and said, 'If the police don't turf you off that island, one of the less friendly street dwellers will,' then proceeded on his way.

We sat in silence as his car disappeared down the road. Eventually, while the day began to dawn around us, I put my hand on my brother's shoulder and said, 'You know what, brother, I'm going to talk to Vikas.'

'About being a ragpicker?'

'About being a ragpicker.'

'Can I be one too?'

'If that is what you really want,' I said. I knew that I couldn't leave him on his own. That's what I found the most difficult. It was one thing to get myself into the situation where I had to pick though other people's rubbish, but I had reduced my brother to the same. We had been so proud to go to school while other children looked on, because we knew that one day it would lead us to a good job. We had watched our father in his office and aspired to be like him. Now here we were, dirty, hungry and tired, and desperate to do anything that would earn us enough money to buy our next meal.

'You bet,' Sandeep said cheerfully. 'It'll be cool, and anything's better than just wandering round the streets starving all day long.'

He meant it too. He was really keen to get started, so as soon as it was properly light we set off on the long walk to the city dump. When we arrived, though, we couldn't find Vikas anywhere. We scoured the whole area, but there was no sign of him.

'Perhaps he's gone to empty his sack somewhere,' Sandeep suggested.

'Maybe he doesn't start till late,' I said.

We sat down on a rock and waited. The tip was even busier than it had been on the Sunday. Trucks were arriving and dumping more rubbish, which caused a frenzy of activity as men, women and children vied with each other to be the first to sift through it. I wondered how it must feel to dig your hands into other people's mess, and quickly pushed the thought of it out of my mind. The smell from close up must be absolutely foul. I couldn't imagine walking over it with bare feet like most of the ragpickers were doing.

I began to think that Vikas wasn't going to be there that day, which caused me a mixture of relief and anxiety. I was so happy that we weren't going to be joining the band of ragpickers crawling over the dump, but because of the dog we hadn't yet eaten and I was beginning to feel lightheaded with hunger again.

'He's not coming,' I said, standing up. 'Let's go and see if we can find him.'

We couldn't find him, of course. We didn't really know where to look. I had some wild hope that we would bump into him simply because we wanted to see him. But in a large, still unfamiliar city teeming with people and with streets going off in all directions, there was little chance. We had no idea of his regular haunts, apart from the fact that once we had found him at the dump and once on a building site playing cricket. Our only other meeting had been when he had found us.

It wasn't long before Sandeep complained about being hungry, and then he stopped in the middle of a street and refused to go any further unless I found him something to eat.

'It's just as bad for me,' I hissed.

'No it's not,' he argued. 'It's not as bad for you because you're older. And you decided to run away, not me, and now I want to go home because nothing's as bad as this, not even Appa.'

'You know that's not true,' I said. 'You know we couldn't stay. I thought we were in this together.'

'I don't want to be in it any more. I hate it here. I hate being hungry and I want to see Amma.'

He was close to breaking down completely and passers-by were staring at us, one or two of them glaring at me as if they thought I were bullying him.

'Come on, Sandeep,' I coaxed. 'All we've got to do is find Vikas and we'll be all right again.'

'We're never going to find him. We'll starve to death before we find him.'

I was wishing that he would stop being so melodramatic when I noticed a woman watching us intently. I immediately thought she might be someone in authority and made an attempt to calm my brother. He plonked himself down on the ground and stubbornly crossed his arms.

'You can't sit there, Sandeep,' I implored. 'You're in everybody's way.'

'I don't care,' he said. 'I'm going to stay here until you promise to take me home.'

'I can't promise that.'

The woman stepped towards us as I stood over him in complete despair. 'Here, take this,' she said. She delved into her bag and pulled out a five-rupee piece. 'You're to spend it on food,' she continued, 'nothing else, and then I suggest that you take yourselves off home. The streets are no place for children.' She held the coin out to me. I hesitated to take it, then saw my brother's face and put out my hand.

'Thank you very much,' I murmured. 'Thank you.'

The woman nodded and walked away. Sandeep jumped quickly to his feet. 'What shall we buy?' he cried. 'Come on, let's go and get something.'

I watched the woman disappear into the crowd. 'Have you noticed how every time we become really desperate, something turns up,' I said.

Sandeep looked at me as if I were going mad. 'Just as well,' he said impatiently.

'First there was the jack fruit, then the woman with the coconuts, then the man with the puris, then the pizzas, and now this.'

'And I found the chicken except that you threw it away, and Arun brought you a drink and Vikas gave us some of his biriani. Now come on, or I'll take that money from you.'

We headed for a stall that sold puris and sambar sauce. The thought of freshly cooked food made my mouth tingle. I watched, mesmerised, as the stallholder fried the little rounds of white dough in front of our eyes. I held out our five rupees and wondered how many that would buy us. The man dropped six spoonfuls of the mixture on to the griddle. I willed them to rise like balloons. As soon as they were ready, he put them into a bag and handed them to us with a pot of sambar. We didn't wait this time to find a special place for our meal. We dived in straight away and ate it walking along the road, not caring that the sambar ran down our chins and all over our fingers.

When we had finished, we set off in search of the building site where we had played cricket. After several wrong turns, we at last found ourselves on the road leading up to it and were elated when we heard the sound of a ball being hit followed by loud cheers. We came to the gap in the fence and climbed through it. There were even more boys there than at the previous gathering. One of them looked about the same age as Sandeep. He seemed to perk up on seeing my brother and came running towards us.

'Have you come to play?' he asked.

'Looks like it,' said Sandeep, trying to sound cool.

'That's good,' said the boy. 'I'm Chintu. What's your name?'

'Sandeep, and my brother's Suresh.'

I nodded hello, but was concerned that Vikas didn't appear to be there. Arun was batting. As soon as he saw us he called out, 'Hey, islanders, are you going to stand there all day or are you going to do some work?'

Sandeep immediately ran to a position in the field. I looked around again, checking that I hadn't missed Vikas. He wasn't there.

'You playing or not?' Arun demanded.

'Do you know where Vikas is?' I asked.

'Word has it he's been banged up.'

'What do you mean?'

'Police didn't like the look of him and gave him a bed for the night,' Arun sniggered.

'What did he do?'

'Sneezed, I expect, or trod on the wrong bit of pavement. Can we get on with our game or are you going to keep asking questions until it's too dark to see?'

I took up a place in the field, but as far away from the wicket as possible. I wanted to keep my distance from Arun. He was making the most of Vikas's absence, hogging the batting and ordering everyone around. The others seemed to accept it, but I lost interest in playing when he called me a cripple because I failed to stop a ball that was going to the boundary. Straight afterwards he gave the bat to Sandeep and told him to have a go. My brother was like a dog with two tails. He strutted over to the wicket, marked the crease and fidgeted his feet until he was in position. Arun handed the ball to Chintu.

'Let's see who's the best of the little boys,' he grinned.

Chintu rubbed the ball to a shine, asked Sandeep if he was ready, then started his run-up. He bowled, Sandeep prepared to take an almighty swipe, the ball spun wickedly, Sandeep missed, and it rolled into the makeshift stumps.

'Out!' cried Chintu. 'Out first ball!'

'Great bowling, young man,' said Arun. 'Bad luck, little islander.'

Sandeep was furious. 'It wasn't fair, I wasn't ready,' he protested. 'Let me have another go.'

'The rules of cricket say that when you're out you're out. So you're out,' Arun insisted. 'It's big brother's turn.'

'He can have my turn,' I said quickly.

'You can't just change the rules,' countered Arun.

'I don't mind if he has another go,' said Chintu. 'It was a bit of a funny bounce.'

'Let him have another go,' a voice came from behind us.

We spun round to see Vikas walking towards us. As he drew nearer I noticed a gash on his cheekbone and a swelling under his eye.

'You weren't here so we're doing what I say,' Arun challenged. 'Hey, what happened to you?'

'He's new here and he's a baby. Why don't we give him a chance?'

'I'm not a baby,' protested Sandeep.

'Don't just ignore me,' said Arun, paying no attention to my brother. 'What happened to your face?'

I could sense Arun's hostility mounting. Vikas put his hand to his face and shrugged his shoulders. 'It's nothing. They gave the beggar a harder time.'

'You need to learn to stop antagonising those brutes.'

'I didn't do anything. They just pounced on me when I was going through some rich man's rubbish. It's always the same two. The rest are all right.'

'They're all a bunch of baboons if you ask me,' Arun said dismissively. 'I wouldn't trust any of them.'

'Are you going to let the little kid bat on or not?' asked Vikas.

'I don't want to bat any more,' said Sandeep, throwing the bat to the ground.

I kept my head down too. Seeing Vikas's face and hearing what had happened to him, I was horrified now at the thought of becoming a ragpicker.

The game finished when darkness fell and I was grateful to get away. I headed quickly for the fence, but Vikas caught us up. 'How are you doing?' he asked. 'Sorry about Arun being so bossy.'

'He was right though,' I risked saying. 'If you're out you should accept it.'

'It was a flukey ball,' protested Sandeep.

'Have you thought any more about ragpicking?' Vikas asked. He saw me look at his face. 'It's no big deal,' he said. 'It's only happened to me once before. You just have to keep your eyes open and stay out of the way of those policemen who can't control their fists. Anyway, most of them ignore us because we're the only ones doing anything about clearing the streets.' Vikas said it with something like pride in his voice.

'Did the police beat you up?' Sandeep butted in. 'Our father –'

131

'What would we have to do?' I cut him short.

'Nobody's collecting glass on my patch at the moment. The kid who used to do it has moved over to a different patch because he wanted to do plastic.'

'What do you mean "your patch"? Don't you work on the rubbish tip?'

'Only when I wake up late,' Vikas grinned.

I didn't know what he meant but there were other things I wanted to ask. 'Where do you work, then?'

'I've got a few streets that are mine. I sort out aluminium cans from the rubbish that people leave there. I'm lucky because there are quite a few rich people living in my patch and they leave a better sort of rubbish.'

'Don't they mind?'

'Why should they? It means there's not so much of it lying around outside their houses until the trucks decide to turn up. And some of them think it's good that we separate it all out.'

'What do you do with it when you've collected it?' It was an obvious question, but one that I had only just thought to ask.

'Sell it, of course,' he laughed. 'What else would I do with it?'

'People pay money for it?' Sandeep said incredulously.

'Dealers do. Then they sell it on to companies who can recycle it. I'll introduce you. Are you in or out?'

'I'm in,' said Sandeep without even looking at me. 'When do we start?'

'What about you, big brother?' Vikas looked at me searchingly. I didn't have any choice, he knew that. He held out his hand and I shook it. 'I'll pick you up at five o'clock tomorrow morning. See ya.' He darted off along the road before I could say anything else.

Chapter 14

'You ready to get your hands dirty?' Vikas stood over us, grinning broadly, as he woke us the next morning.

I dragged myself from a deep sleep and sat up. It was still dark. 'What time is it?' I asked.

'Half past four,' he replied. 'The earlier we are the richer the pickings, and I couldn't sleep, unlike some people.'

I shook Sandeep by the shoulder. He grunted a protest and wasn't about to move until Vikas warned him that he wouldn't eat if he didn't work.

'How long have you been here now?' he asked us as we set off along the road.

I had to think hard. The days all seemed to have blurred into one. 'About a week,' I said.

'Have you found anywhere to wash yet?'

I shook my head.

'Thought not,' he snorted, turning up his nose.

I didn't think he smelt that great himself, but I didn't say anything. He walked very fast. It was difficult to keep up with him. There were the usual piles of rubbish outside shops and houses along the way, but we hurried past all of them. I wondered why we couldn't just stop and sift through any of them. Nobody else seemed to be about so early. Sandeep voiced my thoughts when he stopped to complain that he was puffed out.

'Why can't we just take any of this rubbish? Why do we have to go so far?'

'Doesn't belong to us,' said Vikas, hurrying us on again. 'This patch belongs to a woman called Meera. I wouldn't want to upset her. She's got a tongue like a viper. Anyway, we don't trespass on each other's patches.'

We kept on going, not without more grumbles from my brother. Once, I caught a fleeting glimpse of someone delving into the rubbish behind an office block. Another time, I saw an old man picking through the bottles left in a crate outside a restaurant. He lifted each one to his mouth before putting them into his sack. Vikas called out to him that it must be his lucky day, but I couldn't understand the reply. A young girl, not much older than Sandeep, was standing on a corner. Vikas was about to give her some money and tell her to go back to bed, when he saw a man emerge from the shadows, a threatening look on his face. He put the money back in his pocket and urged us to move on.

At last, he turned down a side street and told us that it marked the beginning of his patch.

'Is it just this street?' Sandeep wanted to know.

Vikas grinned at him. 'I wouldn't make much money from just one street. My patch spreads over about fifteen kilometres.'

'What, every single street in a fifteen kilometre area?' I gasped.

'No, not every single street.' Vikas grinned again. 'That would take me for ever. The ones I do are a bit dotted about, though.'

I struggled to make sense of what he was saying. I realised that if we had had to start on our own we would have been in all sorts of trouble by now, especially with viper-tongued women and threatening men lurking in the shadows. I wondered how Vikas had ever marked out his patch in the first place.

'What do we have to do, then?' I asked.

He reached into his own sack and pulled out two more, handing one to each of us. 'You have to fill these up with glass. Not bottles, someone else does bottles, just pieces of glass. And be careful. Don't cut yourselves. The doctors don't want to be bothered with us.'

We followed him round to the back of a row of concrete houses. There were piles of rotting rubbish in the yard behind them. 'We're the first today,' he said as he began to pick his way through a cardboard box piled high with a mixture of food remains, paper and something quite unrecognisable. He whooped triumphantly when he came across an aluminium can, trod on it to flatten it, then lobbed it into his open sack. 'Come on,' he said. 'You won't find anything if you just stand there. Get stuck in.'

Sandeep and I looked at each other. There was nothing else for it. I bent over a plastic bag that was spilling out over the ground. Sandeep headed for a tall bin. I put my hand in ever so carefully, then shrieked as a rat shot out and disappeared across the yard.

'I was wrong,' laughed Vikas. 'We're not the first. Sorry, I forgot to mention the rats.'

'Made me jump,' I muttered.

'Not as much as you made him jump,' Vikas hooted. 'His fur was standing up on end.'

I grinned in spite of myself, but I kicked the bag with my foot before I put my hand inside it again. I wished I had some gloves. I wished too that I had a face mask as I felt around. I had no idea what I was putting my hands into, and the smell was awful. I tried not to think about what diseases I might be exposing myself and my brother to.

I didn't find anything solid in that first bag. I stood up and stretched my back.

'Catch!' called Vikas.

Something flashed across my face and clattered to the ground. It was a piece of glass.

'Just as well you can't catch, or you'd have cut your hand,' he chuckled.

'I can catch,' I protested. 'I caught you out when we played cricket.'

'That was a fluke, wasn't it, Sandeep?'

Sandeep was on tiptoe and bent double over the bin, one arm pushed deep inside it. He straightened up long enough to say, 'Yeah, that was a fluke,' then started to burrow again.

'Thanks for the support,' I said grumpily.

'Hey, lighten up, big brother,' said Vikas. 'It's only a bit of banter.'

I tried to brush it off, but I didn't like being made to look foolish in front of Sandeep, and I didn't like it when my little brother took sides against me. I slouched off to a big box of rubbish a few doors away from where Vikas and Sandeep were searching. I dug into it, savagely, until at last I'd calmed down a bit and realised that I was being ridiculous.

'Found anything good to eat yet?' I called, 'because if not you can share this with me.' I held out a chapatti that was green with mould.

'Ugh!' cried Sandeep. 'No fear.'

'Funny how I don't feel hungry at the moment,' said Vikas.

And then I found a large piece of glass. 'Hey, look what I've got,' I called. I waved it in the air. My feeling of elation was as great as when I'd caught that cricket ball. I'd made a start on my new career. I put it carefully into my sack and delved in the box with renewed energy.

I soon discovered, though, as did Sandeep, that collecting broken glass was far from rewarding. While Vikas regularly added another can to his hoard, we struggled to find much at all. We'd already picked our way through several streets and still had only a smattering of glass in each of our sacks.

'No wonder that other kid decided to collect plastic instead,' I said rubbing my back, which was sore from bending over. 'We could do better with plastic.'

'Someone else does plastic here. Plastic's popular because there's lots of it and it doesn't weigh very much. Bottles are even worse than glass. There aren't many of them because people reuse them, and if you do find any they weigh a ton.'

By now, the sun was up and I began to notice more and more children flitting through the gaps in between buildings. I probably wouldn't have seen them at all if I hadn't become one of their number. It was as if we inhabited a shadow world, hidden away like some guilty secret behind the acceptable face of the city. Yet we were doing a job that made life in the city more tolerable, shifting huge amounts of rubbish from the streets. Sandeep and I were now part of this vast recycling machine, and without us the city would have suffocated beneath its waste. It made me feel as though I had some worth, and I began to see why Vikas could strut around with such a sense of self-importance, even if some members of the police thought that his only value was as a punchbag.

I was relieved when, after what seemed like hours, Vikas stopped at a corner shop, disappeared inside, then came out again holding a bunch of bananas, a bag of cakes and a bottle of water. 'Breakfast,' he announced. It felt more like lunchtime, we had been up for so long. We followed him to a small side street lined with trees and sat down underneath one of them, our backs leaning up against it. 'Don't expect this every day,' Vikas said, as we munched our way hungrily through bananas. 'You'll have to feed yourselves as soon as you get paid.' I told him how grateful we were, but secretly wondered, looking at my near-empty sack, how we would ever have any money to buy our own food.

While we were sitting there, I asked Vikas why he was living on the streets and how long he had been there. He told us that when his mother had died, his father had taken another wife, and that once they'd had another baby the new wife didn't want him around. He had been living on the streets for three years, since he was twelve. When he was living at home, he had only gone to school erratically because his father expected him to contribute to the family income by working on his coconut plantation.

'Can you read?' Sandeep asked before I could stop him.

'Enough to get by,' said Vikas.

'Will you stay on the streets for ever?' my brother asked then.

'One day, I shall run my own business selling motorbikes, and as soon as I'm sixteen I'm going to ask for a job with a motorbike dealer. Even if I have to start off by cleaning bikes until they are sold, I will be happy with that because I will be able to learn all about them.' He said it almost as if he had learnt it word for word, like a speech.

'What if they won't give you a job?' Sandeep was determined to keep probing.

'They will, I know they will. I've got a friend who's promised to help me. In ten months' time I'll stop being a ragpicker.'

I was impressed by his certainty, but hoped it wouldn't be three years before I could get Sandeep back to school and myself into some sort of training for a good job. After just a few hours, I was convinced I wouldn't last as a ragpicker.

We were about to set off again, when Chintu arrived with another boy, whom he introduced as Tej. I recognised him as one of the cricketers.

'Are you doing Vikas's patch with him?' Chintu asked us.

I nodded while Sandeep shifted uncomfortably, probably remembering what had happened in the cricket.

'I thought you might,' he smiled. 'Not the best, though, is it, glass? I do paper. It's not so heavy and there's more of it.'

'They've got to start somewhere,' Vikas butted in. 'They can't expect to come in at the top.'

'Tej collects bones, but not on the same patch, don't you, Tej?'

The boy nodded.

'Tej can't speak,' Chintu informed us. 'He's amazing at music, though. Are you coming to the party to-night?'

I looked at Vikas for some sort of translation.

'There's a big empty room at the back of a derelict building. We go there sometimes to play music and have a laugh,' he explained.

'Can we come?' Sandeep asked.

'If you're not tucked up in bed by then,' Vikas grinned. 'And if we've finished our round. Come on, we've been sitting here for long enough.'

'See you later,' said Chintu cheerfully.

'See you later,' said Vikas.

Chapter 15

We watched the city wake up around us as we moved from one pile of rubbish to the next, and as it woke up I found myself longing for the night-time, when I could curl up in a ball on our island and sleep. I was amazed at how Vikas and his friends managed to stay so cheerful. Well before we stopped in the middle of the day, my back was aching, my feet were sore, and I felt as if the foul smells that came from the rubbish had sunk into every pore of my body. Vikas's sack was nearly full by then. Mine was still less than a quarter full, and Sandeep's was about the same. Even so, they were beginning to weigh heavily over our drooping shoulders.

I was so relieved when at last Vikas said that we could finish for the morning. Then he told us we had to wash everything that we had collected.

'You'll be able to wash yourselves while you're at it,' he chuckled.

'Why do we have to wash everything?' Sandeep wanted to know.

'The scrap dealers won't touch it if it's not clean,' Vikas replied as we traipsed after him along a narrow back street. 'They wouldn't want to risk getting diseased or anything.'

'Where do we go to wash it?'

'There's a bit by the canal where you can get right close to the water. Some of us go there, some go to an old tap in the railway yard, some go to the fire station and bribe one of the firemen, some go to the tannery, and some use the tap by the slum.'

We continued in silence for a while. Vikas was still walking fast and Sandeep was dropping further and further behind. I tried to bridge the gap between them, but even I found it impossible to keep up with the pace Vikas was setting.

'Come on, you two,' he said impatiently. 'My dealer won't wait for us if we're not there on time.'

I was worried that the dealer might decide we weren't good enough at our job and tell Vikas to find someone else, though at that particular moment, if it meant that I could lie down, I might have been overjoyed at the decision. I knew that Sandeep, who had started off more enthusiastically than I had, was already fed up. I knew, too, that we couldn't give up after one morning. If the other boys could cope, then surely it couldn't be that bad. Perhaps it was just a question of getting used to it. Perhaps when we had done it for long enough, our feet and our backs would no longer ache. Perhaps we wouldn't notice the stench after a while. Even the rats and dogs might leave us alone. And the cattle. I had had to compete with an ox for one big box of rubbish, and I didn't like the look in its eye.

At last, Vikas turned a corner and in front of us was the canal. It was very narrow and overgrown. When we peered over the edge we saw that it, too, was awash with rubbish. The smell was unbelievable as it rotted in the heat of the midday sun.

'Stinks!' Sandeep exclaimed, dropping his sack and putting his hands over his face.

'Half the waste from the city goes straight into this canal,' Vikas informed us.

'I thought you said we could wash in it,' I said.

He ignored me and led us along the embankment towards a small bridge. To the side of it was a large area of worn ground, which sloped gently down to a part of the canal wall that had collapsed. We weren't the first to arrive. More than a dozen adults and children were already sitting by the water's edge. Some younger children were splashing around in the water, while a number of adults were scrubbing their clothes.

'Are they all ragpickers?' I asked.

'Most of them,' replied Vikas. 'The little ones help their mothers.'

We drew closer, and I could see that several of the children were only about four or five years old. One of them was picking up pieces of glass that his mother had cleaned, and holding them up to watch them glisten in the sun. Vikas greeted everyone with smiles and jokes, before introducing us as part of his team. I enjoyed the feeling of being welcomed into what seemed like a great big family. It reminded me of the days when at festival time all the people in our village would gather on the banks of the river to celebrate. We made our way to a spot close to the water and sat down. It was such a relief not to have to carry our sacks for a while. We emptied them on to the ground and began the process of cleaning each piece.

It would have been so easy to stretch out and go to sleep on that canal bank. The sun beat down on us, the conversations were loud and animated, the stench from the water made us feel sick, yet we were so tired, Sandeep and I, that we could have slept through it all. Vikas kept us to our task, though, insisting that we wash off every last bit of dirt and grime, and telling us that if we didn't go voluntarily into the water to wash ourselves he would push us in.

'We'll be even filthier if we go in there,' I protested.

'Just make sure you walk out to the middle where the water's flowing. It'll freshen you up and you won't smell as bad. And if you don't hurry up, I won't take you to the dealer.'

He pushed past us and ran into the water himself. Sandeep and I looked at each other, took off our shoes, then plunged forwards, heading for the middle of the canal as quickly as we could to avoid the rotting mess that clung to the edges. Once there, we were glad to discover that the water seemed a lot cleaner. Vikas began to splash us as soon as we were close enough to him.

'I'll soon get you clean,' he laughed.

'We'll soon clean you too,' I laughed back.

That was the signal to launch into a huge waterfight. Other children ran from the bank to join us. The misery of the morning vanished in an avalanche of drops. It was the most fun we had had since leaving home and we didn't want it to end. I ducked down under the water and swished my hair around. I felt so refreshed when I resurfaced. I was about to do it again when Vikas signalled that it was time to leave.

'Do we have to?' Sandeep grumbled, but he followed me out.

We climbed up the side of the bank, shook ourselves off and went to put on our shoes.

They weren't there.

We searched all around in case we were mistaken about where we had put them. They were nowhere to be found. The feeling that we had been welcomed into a big family was destroyed in an instant with the realisation that somebody in that family had stolen our shoes. Vikas asked the people who were still sitting there if anyone had seen anything, but we encountered nothing but blank looks and shaken heads.

'Someone might have kicked them into the water,' Sandeep offered, trying to peer through the scum. I think we all knew that that wasn't what had happened.

'I reckon it was the boys who were gambling under the bridge,' said Vikas. 'I've never seen them before, but I'll know them if I see them again.'

'Especially if they're wearing our shoes,' I said grimly.

'Does that mean we'll have to go barefoot?' Sandeep asked. I could hear the complaint in his voice already.

'Looks like you haven't got any choice,' said Vikas. 'Join the club.'

'It's all right for you,' my brother retorted. 'Your feet are used to it.'

'And yours are all soft and shiny and you don't want to spoil them,' scoffed Vikas. He ruffled my brother's hair. 'I know it's tough,' he said, 'but you're street kids now, and if you don't get used to living like street kids you won't survive.'

I knew he was right, but I was devastated that we had been robbed of the one thing that really separated us from the other street kids and kept alive my hope that I would soon have a better job. We could somehow pretend to be different all the while we had a good pair of shoes on our feet. How would we manage without them? It would take a long time for our feet to become hardened. I couldn't imagine how we would cope walking along baking hot streets, let alone scrambling over rotting heaps of rubbish full of pieces of metal and glass.

Vikas clearly didn't think it was a problem. 'Come on,' he said, 'we've wasted enough time.'

We trundled after him, walking gingerly across an area of hot, sharp gravel, Sandeep moaning in my wake. It made me feel guilty again, and I was fed up with feeling guilty. I wondered how far we had to walk to reach the dealer, and how much he would give us for our pathetic haul.

Vikas, as if reading my thoughts, turned to say, 'Hurry up, it's not far. Just think about the money.'

'It's thinking about that that's worrying me,' I said ruefully.

'Whatever he gives you it'll be better than nothing, but he won't pay you until we've finished today.'

I stopped in my tracks. 'What do you mean?' I asked.

'We've got another three hours to go yet. When we've washed whatever we get then and taken it to him he'll pay us for the whole lot.'

'Why can't he pay us now?' said Sandeep. 'What if he won't pay us later on?'

'It's his rules,' said Vikas. 'We don't have a choice.'

I hadn't expected that. I cursed myself for not having asked more questions before we had started out that morning. At least then we would have known what we were letting ourselves in for. I didn't want to work for another three hours. I was too exhausted. I didn't want to wait to be paid. How would I have any idea of the value of what we had collected if we weren't paid straight away? The waterfight had been fun but because of it we had lost our shoes. It was good to feel clean, but what was the point if we were going to crawl through more rubbish so soon afterwards?

I could tell Vikas that we were not going to do any more until the next day. I could tell him that we needed time to get used to the work. I could ask the dealer to pay us for the morning session because we weren't going to continue that day. But then I thought how pathetic it would be if we gave up after half a day. The other ragpickers managed. Even Chintu kept going, with a big smile on his face, and he was at least two years younger than me.

We were entering a part of the city that I wouldn't have ventured into on my own. The streets were narrow, dark and crowded with shabby, decaying buildings. Men were hanging around in doorways chewing paan or gambling in small groups on their verandahs. Small children were playing with stones in the gutters, their clothes in rags. There was none of the colour that we were used to seeing amongst even the poorest families in my village. In this decaying area of the city, the women's saris were dull and their faces drawn and lifeless. The slum outside the city didn't seem as gloomy and threatening, even though the poverty there was the worst I had ever seen. Perhaps it was because there were open spaces all around, even if they were mostly barren. Perhaps it was the red and yellow jugs the women carried to and fro, the clothing laid out on the rocks to dry, and the coloured tarpaulins that were strewn across their crude huts to provide shelter.

Vikas wove his way expertly in and out of the gangs of children, who stared at us with vacant eyes or challenged us with unpleasant names. When they were out of earshot, Vikas called them names as well. 'Those scum look down on us because of what we do,' he said. 'Morons like that prefer to beg and steal rather than do an honest day's work.' I felt sorry for them, though. Amma had always taught us that nobody, however low their position in life, deserved to live in squalor.

We came to a large, dilapidated building with wide metal doors to the front. To the side was another, smaller door. Vikas rapped loudly on it. We waited but nobody came. Vikas knocked again. This time we heard footsteps and the sound of bolts being pulled back. The door opened slightly. A fat, unshaven face with a beedi hanging from its mouth peered through the gap. 'Bit late, aren't you?' it said.

'Sorry, Mr Roy,' said Vikas. 'I've got two new kids with me. They're a bit slow.'

The face came round the door a bit further and blew a cloud of smoke in our direction. 'Taking them out of the nursery now, are we?'

'They come as a package,' replied Vikas, winking at me. 'And we need some extra hands.'

'Long as they don't go thinking they're better than they are, like the last one did the minute we got him trained up.'

He opened the door wide enough for us to go through it. We found ourselves inside a small ware-house. Lots of big wooden crates were parked on the floor, each one containing a different sort of rubbish. The room was blissfully cool but horribly stale-smelling. Mr Roy led us to the far end, where he had a table and a rusty old till. He was about forty, I guessed. He was wearing a white shirt with food stains down the front. His western-style grey trousers scarcely fitted round his enormous protruding belly. I stared at this man who would be so important to our survival. I didn't like what I saw.

'Let's see what they've got, then,' he said to Vikas.

He indicated that we should empty our sacks into a low metal bowl. He coughed, spat on the floor close by us, then wiped his sleeve across his mouth before puffing again on the beedi. Sandeep and I did as we were told, tipping both of our sacks upside down on to one pile. We shook out every last corner to make sure nothing was stuck. When we had finished, the dealer stood over the bowl and spat again.

'Not much to show for a whole morning's work, is it?' he grunted, again addressing his remark to Vikas.

'They'll get quicker,' Vikas said.

'They'll have to. Not worth the effort, this isn't.'

'How much are you going to pay us?' Sandeep demanded.

'Blimey, it's got the cheek of the devil, the nursery one,' Mr Roy exclaimed. 'It's them what should be paying me for wasting my time.'

'Don't worry, Mr Roy, I'll make sure they bring more stuff next time,' Vikas assured him.

'Yeah, well, I'm not a charity. Anyway, let's have a better look.' He bent down and started to sift through the glass. 'Some of it's not washed properly,' he snapped. 'It's no good to me if it's dirty. They don't expect me to wash it meself, do they?' He picked out one piece after another and threw them to the side.

'There's a tap over there,' he said. 'Get them to clean it again.'

I glared at him but he wouldn't look me in the eye. If he didn't look at me, he could pretend I didn't exist.

'You'd better do as Mr Roy says,' Vikas said firmly, glaring at me in turn. 'Mr Roy can't sell anything that's dirty.'

'Who does he sell it to?' Sandeep asked as the dealer disappeared through a door behind him.

'Anywhere that can recycle it and get a second use from it.'

'Does he make a lot of money from doing that?' Sandeep asked again.

'Shhh,' Vikas warned.

The dealer had reappeared, a fresh beedi pressed between his lips. 'Hurry up and get cleaning, will you?' He pushed a bucket in our direction.

We gathered up the rejected pile, though I wanted to tell the dealer that he could keep his horrible job. While we were at the tap, Vikas emptied out his own sack then came over to us while Mr Roy was checking through it.

'Don't let him get to you,' he whispered. 'He's just testing you out.'

'He could try being a bit more friendly,' I glowered. 'And there was nothing wrong with any of this glass. He's just being fussy.'

'He's in business. He's not going to make it easy for you.'

It irritated me that Vikas was prepared to stand up for a man who, as far as I could see, was nothing but a bully. I was about to say something when Mr Roy called Vikas over.

'They finished yet?' he grunted. 'I've got others to see, you know.'

We shovelled the pieces back into the bucket and returned them for inspection. Mr Roy didn't even look at them. He scribbled something on some paper and showed it to Vikas. 'That's yours,' he said. 'They'll be getting a quarter of that between them, and that's only because I'm feeling generous.'

I tried to see what he had written, but he snatched the paper away. There was a loud rap on the door. He dismissed us without looking up and told Vikas that we had better not take up so much of his time on our next visit. We followed him to the door, waited while he slid back the bolts, and squeezed through the narrow gap as he questioned the identity of the new arrivals. I was too glad to be leaving Mr Roy and his dark and smelly warehouse to catch their names or see their faces, but as the door closed behind them I suddenly realised that one of them was wearing my shoes.

Chapter 16

We couldn't go back into the warehouse. Vikas wouldn't let us. 'How're you going to prove they're yours?' he argued. 'And anyway, that scumbag will sack the lot of us if we get into a fight. He knows there'll soon be others knocking on his door begging to work for him.'

'Who cares if he does sack me?' I shouted. 'That kid had my shoes. I want them back and I want Sandeep's back.'

'Don't expect me to come with you then,' Vikas shouted back. 'If you want to be stupid that's up to you. But you won't get paid for this morning and he could make it difficult for you with the other dealers.'

I was so close to losing my head completely. That day was turning into one of the worst of my life. Why should I care about Mr Roy and the other dealers? They didn't care about me. I didn't need their pathetic job. So what if I didn't get paid for the morning? I could find something else. There had to be better ways to survive. I ran towards the door, ready to pummel it with my fists, but Sandeep caught hold of my arm.

'Don't, Suresh,' he said. 'I don't want you to get into a fight. Let them have our stupid shoes. At least without them we're like all our friends.'

I looked at him in astonishment. What did he mean? All our friends had shoes. And then I realised that he didn't mean the friends we had left behind in our village. He meant Vikas and Chintu, even Arun, and all the other street kids who were running around with nothing on their feet. I couldn't believe that Sandeep, who had followed along behind me complaining bitterly about how sore his feet were, was now announcing that we were better off shoeless. I lowered my arm in defeat.

'What's the point, anyway,' I said. 'They won't give them back.'

'Got it in one,' said Vikas. 'Come on, big brother. You never know, round the corner might be the biggest pile of glass you've ever seen and with it your fortune.'

'Yeah, come on, Suresh. Let's go and find our fortune,' joined in Sandeep.

I snorted loudly. I wasn't in the mood for being jolly. I tramped along behind them, scuffing my feet in the dust and watching it puff up through my toes. I knew that I had to stop being such a misery. Vikas was doing his best for us. Even Sandeep was making an effort in between his complaints. We came to an apartment block. Sandeep whooped with glee when he discovered a box of broken bottles.

'Come on, Suresh,' he hooted. 'It's our fortune!'

With a big effort to look pleased, I helped him to load it into our sacks. Our luck ran out after that, but at least that first find kept us going for the rest of the afternoon, and we ended up with just as much in our sacks as we had collected over the course of the morning.

Instead of going back to the canal, which was a long way from where we had finished up, Vikas took us to a standpipe round the back of a huge old tannery to wash our second collection. We scrubbed so hard at every last piece. I was determined that Mr Roy should have nothing to complain about. I stood defiantly at the warehouse door when Vikas rapped. I was full of confidence that the dealer would be happier with our haul. Sandeep and I were both excited. We were about to be paid the first money we had ever earned in our lives.

It wasn't Mr Roy who opened the door. It was a skinny old man. He only opened it far enough for us to see his squinty eyes, his long hooked nose and blackened, twisted teeth. 'If it's Mr Roy you're wanting he won't be back till the morning,' the man said.

'Where's he gone, Pooran?' Vikas demanded.

'Mr Roy had important business,' the old man whistled through his teeth.

'And he expects us to walk around all night with these sacks, does he?'

'Mr Roy is willing to let you leave your sacks here.'

'How do we know he won't tip out half of what we've collected?'

'Mr Roy is an honourable man.'

'And you're a fool.' Vikas swung his sack back over his shoulder and marched away. 'There's always some reason why he can't pay us,' he snarled. 'I'll get myself a different dealer if he doesn't watch out.'

My heart sank as I understood that this wasn't the first time Mr Roy hadn't paid out the money he owed when it was due. Sandeep took hold of my arm and asked if it meant that we weren't going to eat again. I looked at his despairing face, and wondered how many more knocks we were going to take that day.

We caught up with Vikas and asked him what he was going to do. 'Right at this moment,' he said, 'I'm going to find somewhere to get my head down. And then I'm going to put on my best clothes and go to the party.'

'Aren't you going to eat?' asked Sandeep.

'No money,' he replied. 'I used it this morning. See you later?'

'Is that it?' I asked. 'Do we just let Mr Roy get away with not paying us?'

'Not much we can do if he's not there. I'll sort him out in the morning.' He began to stride away.

'Where is it tonight?' I called after him.

'On the roof next to the tannery. Can you find your way back?'

I nodded and watched as he walked away again. I wondered where he was going until the evening and wished that we could go with him, but I had the feeling that he didn't want us trailing around with him all the time, that he didn't want the responsibility of looking after us. I couldn't blame him, either. He'd already found us a job and spent his last bit of money on us.

There was nothing to be achieved by our hanging around outside the warehouse. Even if Mr Roy did return, I knew that I wouldn't have the nerve to confront him. I was too tired anyway to stay on my feet for much longer, especially since the soles of them were cut and bruised and burnt.

'We'd better get some rest,' I said to Sandeep, 'if we're going out tonight.'

'Aren't we going to eat?' he muttered, but he already knew the answer, and like me he knew that this was how it was going to be, day after day, week after week. Month after month? I hoped not. I so hoped not. We walked back to the building site near our island, hid our sacks under some rubble, and found a piece of flat ground on which to lie down.

We must have fallen asleep straight away, because the next thing I knew I woke up to find that it was dark and the traffic had quietened right down. I sat up and stretched. I could quite happily have gone back to sleep again, even though the ground was hard and lumpy compared to our island, but I liked the idea that we were going out at night. We would never have gone out this late when we were at home, except at festival time when everyone stayed up. I roused Sandeep, who complained that every single bit of his body ached and that his leg was sore where the dog had bitten him. I tried to examine it. I couldn't see anything in the dark, but I promised him that we would wash it thoroughly under the tap by the tannery. He complained then that we had nothing to wear.

'Vikas said he was putting on his best clothes,' he grumbled. 'We haven't got any best clothes and these clothes still stink and I've got fleas.'

As soon as he said it I started to feel itchy and realised that I too had been scratching for the last two days. It hadn't been so bad since our dip in the canal, but the fleas were still there.

'Vikas hasn't got any best clothes either,' I said. 'He was joking.'

Sandeep considered that for a moment, then asked, 'What happens when these clothes get too small?'

'We'll have enough money to buy some new ones by then,' I said confidently.

Sandeep sniffed. He didn't believe me, but he stood up and said that at least we were going to have some fun for a change.

'Yeah,' I agreed. 'Let's go and have some fun.'

We set off along the road arm in arm, alternating between skipping and running, grateful for the fact that at last the pavements were cooler. When we saw a police car coming towards us, we slipped into the shadows until it had gone past. I knew the rough direction in which we needed to head, but we were in danger of getting lost because everything looked so different under the dim street lights. We came to a road where women with small children were arranging their sleeping sheets and bamboo mats for the night. Further along, a group of beggars were gambling in the gutter. One of them held his hand out to us and cursed us as we hurried by. Another road we came to was lined with restaurants, brightly lit and with uniformed doormen standing guard on their steps. We peered through the windows, when the doormen weren't looking, at women in the most beautiful saris and men in smart western suits. A street dweller was trying to set up his cardboard boxes outside a hotel. The hotel manager threatened him with the police if he didn't move on, while the street dweller argued that he deserved a clean bit of pavement because he came from a good background and his status as a street dweller was merely temporary. We came to a small roadside temple in front of which a sadhu knelt, entranced. The statue behind the grille was of Hanuman, the monkey god. We hesitated by it. I wished that we had something to offer him so that he would help us to find a lucky path through life. I closed my eyes anyway and asked him to take care of us.

We walked on, past the railway station which was still bustling with travellers and hawkers even at that time in the evening, past the huge department store we had stared in at during our first day in the city, until we came to the narrower streets leading away from the centre.

A voice from a doorway just ahead made me jump.

'Well, if it isn't the famous islanders,' it said.

Arun stepped out on to the pavement in front of us, followed by two other older boys. He had a bottle of beer in one hand and a beedi in the other. He took a deep puff of the beedi, dropped it on the ground and stamped on it.

'Off to the party, are we?' he asked.

The other boys sniggered.

'That's right,' I said, a knot tightening in my stomach. 'Are you going?'

'Maybe, maybe not. We don't really do parties, do we, my friends?'

'Parties? Little boys' parties? Nah. Not enough action, eh?' one of the boys said.

'You should go,' Sandeep jumped in. 'Chintu says it'll be fun and there'll be music as well.'

'Will there indeed?' mocked Arun. 'Let me see. Chintu Baby on paper and comb, Tej-no-tongue on bones, King Vikas on tin cans, someone else on bottles, and the hoity-toity islanders rattling the old glass, is that it?'

I wanted so much to wipe the silly grin off his face. 'Why do you have to be so sarcastic?' I blurted out.

'Well, well, well, so big brother isn't the weakling I thought he was. There's a little bit of the tiger beating inside him. And there's me thinking it was a bit of the mouse.'

'Eek, eek, eek,' chorused the other boys, breaking into more sniggers.

I took Sandeep's arm and moved forward to go past them. Arun took a step to the side as if to block our way, then made a deep bow and ushered us by.

'Have a good evening, islanders,' he said. 'Maybe see you later.'

'See you later, little boys,' said his friends.

I nodded and walked quickly away. I wished that Vikas had been there. He seemed to know how to handle Arun. I hoped that Arun and his friends wouldn't go to the party. I didn't want to spend the rest of the evening being goaded by them.

We came to a network of narrow alleyways and practically ran through them. We were afraid that someone might be lurking in the dark. Every now and again we could hear laughter close by. I wondered if it came from other partygoers, but at the same time I was worried that it might come from Arun and his friends. And then we began to hear music. We took a number of wrong turns before at last we reached the end of one alley and found ourselves facing the rear of the tannery. The music was much louder now. I could make out the sounds of two instruments, a dohl and a devil chaser. They were coming from the roof of the building on the left, which must once upon a time have been a cinema but was now in disrepair. To the front of it were a number of shallow broken steps, tiled in blues and pinks and greens, which led into the dark recesses of the building. We looked back up again and noticed the lights flickering against the blackness of the sky.

'Are we going in, then?' asked Sandeep.

'We haven't come all this way for nothing,' I grinned.

Chapter 17

We had such a good time, that night on the roof, and made so many new friends. There weren't only ragpickers there. There were shoe-shine boys, car washers, water-sellers, coolies, flower-sellers – about thirty altogether, all of them determined to have the best time of their lives. By the light of three oil lamps, they were dancing, making music with anything that made a noise, playing games, sitting in corners and talking, secure within the low wall that surrounded their rooftop retreat. We were welcomed into the midst of them and instantly made to feel at home. Chintu kept asking us if we were all right and how had our first day been and what did we think of Tej playing his devil chaser and how old were we and were we going to play cricket again. Vikas introduced us to some of the other boys and fetched us some water and biscuits, but otherwise left us to join in where we wanted.

After a while I was happy to sit down and watch everything going on around me. Sandeep danced wildly backwards and forwards, urging me to stop being an old man and get up again. When he'd tired of dancing, he picked up two sticks and started beating out a rhythm on a metal barrel that doubled as a seat. It was good to see him enjoying himself. When he took himself off to a corner of the roof where a group of boys were sitting, I leant back against the wall, slid down on to the ground, and allowed myself to relax into the night.

I woke surprised to find myself on the roof, my back stiff from the position I had been lying in. Sandeep was fast asleep beside me. It was dark but I had no idea what time it was. I sat up, thinking that we should make our way back to our island, and wondering what had happened to everyone else. I heard someone muttering from somewhere close by and turned to see who it was. I could just about make out the form of Tej. How strange, I thought, that he should be dumb during the day yet talk in his sleep. Next to him was Chintu, curled up tightly in a ball. As my eyes grew used to the dark, it became clear that the partygoers were all still there, slumped across each other in little clusters.

I stood up, walked to the edge of the roof and looked out across the silhouetted skyline of the city. It was so peaceful at that moment compared with the cacophony that would begin shortly after dawn. There was the occasional distant rumble of a truck, the yap of a dog, the scuffling of a rat, but nothing more. If only it would stay that way. In the quiet of the night, it was as if none of the daytime chaos existed.

A movement behind me made me turn. Sandeep sat up. I was about to say something to him when his head jerked forward and he was violently sick. I ran over to him, putting my hand on his shoulder as he vomited for a second time. He groaned loudly, rocked backwards and forwards then lay back down. I asked if he was all right. He didn't reply. I leant over him. He was asleep. I was petrified that his sickness was something to do with the dog bite on his leg. I had promised that we would wash it and I had completely forgotten. How could I forget when I was supposed to be looking after him? Should I wake him and take him to get it washed now? I shook him. He groaned, turned over, but didn't wake up. I moved his legs away from the pool of sick. Still he slept on. I decided to wait until morning.

I was about to sit down close by him when another figure stood up and stretched. As it moved towards me, I saw that it was Vikas.

'What's the matter? Couldn't sleep away from the comfort of your island?' he grinned.

'My brother's been sick,' I said.

'I thought he might be,' Vikas observed.

'What do you mean?'

'He was sniffing glue.'

I stared at him incredulously through the darkness. 'What do you mean? Why would he do that? How could he have been?'

'When you were asleep. When he disappeared into the corner.'

I was dumbfounded. Was this true? Was this my fault as well?

'Why didn't you wake me? Why didn't you tell me?' I wanted to hit him. He was supposed to be our friend.

'I tried to but you were dead to the world. And I tried to stop your brother but he ignored me.'

'But why would he do it?'

'To make himself look good? To make himself feel good?'

174

'He was sick!' I was shouting now. 'He nearly threw his guts up.'

'So let's hope he won't try it again. But there's plenty of kids doing it on the streets.'

I couldn't believe Sandeep could be so stupid, even if he didn't know what might happen to him. When Chintu woke at that moment, I wondered if he too had been involved in the glue-sniffing. He seemed his usual self, though, bright-eyed and smiling. He was concerned when he saw that my brother had been sick.

'Wrong food,' he said knowingly. 'Better out than in.'

I saw the glance that passed between him and Vikas and knew that he was aware of what had happened. It made me feel ashamed. I wanted to know who the boys were who had encouraged my brother, but before I could ask, Vikas announced that it was time to go to work. I hadn't even thought about work up until then. I didn't want to think about it either.

'No work, no pay, no food,' Vikas said firmly.

'How can I when my brother's not well?'

'You'll have to leave him here. Mr Roy won't be happy if you don't show up after only one day.'

'*He* didn't show up yesterday,' I said sulkily.

'He does what he likes. We do what he says or we're out.'

'Maybe I don't want to do what he says.'

'That's up to you, but I'm off. I want to eat today.' Vikas pulled his sack from behind a pile of wood, threw it over his shoulder and made for the top of the stairs.

'We haven't got our sacks here,' I cried out.

He turned and shrugged. 'You'll have to fetch them,' he said. 'I can't get any more.' He was about to leave when he came back over. 'Look,' he said, 'I'll help you all I can but I've got myself to look after and I'm not going to baby you or your brother. It's like that with all of us. We're there for each other but we can't carry anyone. I'll give you half an hour while I dump this stuff with Mr Roy and make excuses for you. If you're not back here then, you're on your own.'

He didn't give me a chance to answer and disappeared down the stairs. Some of the other boys were waking up and setting about their days. Others slept on. Were they the ones who had encouraged my brother to sniff glue? Sandeep was still fast asleep. Should I wake him or leave him until I returned? I worried

176

about leaving him in case he was sick again, but we needed to eat that day.

'Tej and I will look after him, won't we, Tej?' Chintu came and stood next to me. Sitting just behind Sandeep, Tej nodded. 'He'll be awake and ready to go by the time you get back,' Chintu smiled.

I had my doubts but decided that I couldn't waste any more time. I set off at a run, taking the stairs two at a time and tearing through the alleyways. It was still dark and there were very few street lights in that part of the city. My lungs were bursting by the time I reached the building site and dug out our bags. Before I went back, I peered across longingly at our island. Already it felt like home. Then I saw something move. Someone was there. Somebody was on our island. I was shocked. How dare they? How dare somebody take our home from us? A deep sense of injustice and anger rose within me. I marched across the road, determined to claim it back. I reached the metal fence and gazed down.

It was Arun. As I stood there he stirred. I was so angry that I didn't think about the possible consequences of waking him up. I shouted his name, my voice seeming to echo through the dawn. He sat up with a start. When he saw me, he grinned.

'You're on my island,' I said.

'Correction,' he replied. 'It belongs to the city, this does.'

'You know what I mean.'

'It's very comfy. Much comfier than my bit of pavement.'

'Tough. I was here first.'

'The tiger's out tonight, then,' he said, looking me straight in the eye, challenging me to back down.

'Are you you going to leave?' I tried to sound as threatening as I could.

'All right, all right. No need to get huffy. It was empty so I borrowed it. I wasn't going to let a comfy little number like this go to waste.'

'I want you to leave now,' I growled.

'I'll leave when I'm good and ready,' he countered. 'But be careful, islander. I'll have me this island for good if you neglect it again.'

I glared at him. He lay down and ignored me. I had no choice but to hope that he would leave. He wasn't going to go just because I told him to, and it was time I got back to Sandeep and Vikas. I ran across the road to fetch our sacks, threw them over my shoulder and tried to prepare myself for another day's work. As I set off, I glanced at the island and saw Arun wave goodbye.

* * *

When I got back, all of the other boys had gone except for Vikas, Chintu, Tej and Sandeep. Sandeep was awake. Chintu was fussing around him and had made him drink some bottled water as well as cleaning his leg, which Sandeep accused me of ignoring.

'It's all full of pus,' he said. 'Chintu says it's septic because he's seen septic cuts before. Vikas says I need to keep it clean.'

I wanted to tell him what I thought of him, how stupid he had been, how ashamed Amma would be if she knew, but I didn't want to embarrass him in front of the others, and I knew that some of my anger was aimed at myself because yet again I had failed to take care of him properly.

I looked at Vikas, who shrugged his shoulders and said Sandeep's leg should be all right. He was anxious to begin his day. I didn't tell him about Arun because I didn't want him to think that I was expecting him to do something about it. 'Was Mr Roy there?' I asked.

He nodded but he didn't seem himself. I wondered if Mr Roy had paid him less than he was due. I determined to be as positive as I could that day so as not to annoy our friend any further. He was doing his best for us. I wanted to do my best for him.

I told Sandeep that we needed to start work, half expecting him to refuse, but he stood up, took his sack from me and asked what we were waiting for. I glared at him and hissed that if he ever went anywhere near glue again I wouldn't be responsible for my actions.

That second day followed pretty much the same pattern as the first, except that by the time we reached the canal our sacks were twice as heavy because we were carrying the previous afternoon's collection. Vikas's sack was already full, even though he had emptied it in the morning. We found one piece of glass to every ten cans that Vikas dropped into his sack, yet there were two of us. What was worse was that when we took our booty to Mr Roy, he charged us for the loan of his sacks, as well as keeping some money back as an insurance that we would not do all our training with him and then go to work for someone else.

'You boys are all the same,' he said. 'Not a scrap of loyalty amongst you. I've learnt not to trust you, so this is just my little way of protecting myself.'

He handed over five rupees for our first two days' work, scarcely enough to buy ourselves one meal, and I had hoped to have enough to treat Vikas. There was no point in arguing with him. He would use any excuse not to pay us what we were due. Vikas told us to go to him with no expectations and then everything would seem like a bonus.

'Why don't you work for another dealer?' I asked him.

'Because they're all the same,' he replied, 'and because he owes me money.'

At least Sandeep and I weren't the only ones.

Chapter 18

We staggered through our first weeks. We struggled to get used to the routine of waking up before the sun and not bedding down until the city was already asleep. Arun came by twice to check that we were holding on tight to our island. He took pleasure in taunting me, but I didn't think he had any real intention of taking it from us, if only because, as he gleefully told us, when the monsoon came, and it would soon, we would have to move. I decided to worry about that when the time came. There were plenty of other things to cope with first. Our feet were beginning to harden up and our backs stopped protesting quite so much from being bent double most of the day. Our hands were covered in cuts, the skin was rough and ingrained with dirt and our nails were torn. Amma had always cut our nails so neatly and insisted that we look after our hands if we didn't want to be mistaken for labourers. I had seen the hands of some of the village children who worked in the fields. Ours were like that after just a few days. Sandeep's leg was still raw but it wasn't getting any worse, though I was anxious about him bathing in the dirty canal. Whenever we were near the tannery we washed ourselves under the tap as thoroughly as we could. It was so hot that our clothes were dry within a few minutes, and we would have been happy to douse ourselves over and over again.

Vikas kept us going whenever we showed signs of flagging. He scrambled from one pile of rubbish to another, whooping with glee every time he found a can for himself, a piece of glass for us, or something unexpected like a coin, the remains of a meal, or an article of clothing. Things that were of no value to the person who had thrown them away were sometimes like buried treasure to us. When I found a two-rupee piece, I was so excited that I did a mad dance up and down the street. When Sandeep found an old watch that didn't work, it was as if he had discovered a chest full of gold dust. He put it on his wrist, though it was much too big, and wouldn't be parted from it. The possibility of finding something that would improve our lives became a huge incentive for us to search every inch of every bag of rubbish that we came across. It made such a difference to our state of mind, and helped us to approach our work much more positively.

By the end of the week, and we worked every day, Sandeep and I had been paid a total of twenty rupees between us. Vikas had been paid sixty-five. I didn't begrudge him because he always shared his food with us, but I wished that we could earn more and not have to rely on him. I wished too that we could earn enough to save some for days when, because of illness or the weather, we couldn't work. Vikas told us that he had some savings hidden somewhere and that we should do the same, but I couldn't see how we would ever be in a position to put money aside all the while we were having to collect glass.

Sometimes we gazed through the windows of shops in the city centre, particularly at those that sold shoes. Without shoes I knew I would never be able to get a proper job, but I would not be able to afford a pair of shoes if I didn't have a proper job. It had all seemed so possible when I made the decision to leave home. We would arrive in a town or a city, I would walk straight into a job because I was good at maths and could write well, I would quickly have enough money to send

Sandeep to school, and we would find somewhere to live. How different the reality was.

At least we had our friends. Chintu popped up all over the place to ask if we were all right and to tell us tales of what was happening on the streets. He seemed to know everyone and everything that was going on. I had never met anyone who was so eternally cheerful. Even when he had the worst of days, he just brushed it off and said the next day would be better. 'What's to be sad about?' he would ask. 'The sun is shining, I have my friends, I am not starving, and one day I will own my own restaurant where all my friends can come and eat for free.' It was Chintu who always knew when and where there would be a gathering to play music or cards or cricket. He made sure to tell us and looked after us once we were there. 'It's hard on the streets when you're new,' he kept saying. 'We all help each other here.'

Tej never left Chintu's side. He was like a permanent shadow, never smiling, never speaking, but listening and taking everything in. He only came alive when he was playing music. His whole body moved with the rhythm, his eyes grew wide, his feet tapped urgently. Sometimes he seemed to go into a trance, Chintu said, escaping to another world.

We didn't see much of Arun. Vikas said he was too busy with his robber friends to spend time with us. 'He thinks he's better than us because he doesn't have to work, but one day he'll come unstuck.'

Arun pooh-poohed it when Vikas said as much to him. 'I'm not the one who's had his face used as a punchbag,' he sniffed. 'So I reckon I'm doing better than you are.'

'Doesn't mean it won't be worse for you if you do get caught,' Vikas retorted.

'I'm never gonna get caught and that's a fact,' Arun grinned. 'Those pussy-footed police are too slow-witted for the likes of me.' Arun did what he wanted, when he wanted, but even he, I realised, would drop everything to help a fellow street dweller. However much I might have taken a dislike to him, he had come to my rescue when I had been ill. And he seemed to harbour a grudging respect for Vikas, who was able to make him toe the line when necessary. Vikas, I think, had a sneaking respect for Arun as well, though he would never have admitted it.

Sandeep and I gradually began to feel part of their world. We also began to need them less to help us survive. Little by little, as the city became familiar to us, we found our own ways to deal with hunger and to pass the time when we weren't working. There were plenty of people who objected to the existence of street dwellers and who cursed us if we got in their way. We learned to disappear into the background as much as possible. But there were others who felt sorry for us and tried to help us in whatever small way they could, even if they were struggling to eke out a living themselves.

The man who had given us his leftover puris when we first arrived in the city, once he realised that we had no home to go to, made a point of saving us two every Saturday afternoon. He told us that his name was Bharat Gupta. He had been a bookseller until his shop had been burned down in a riot, when one of the rioters had taken exception to the title of a book in the window. 'It was a cookery book with a strange title,' Bharat chuckled. 'I think he thought it was anti-free speech!' He couldn't afford to rebuild his business and had been selling puris ever since. 'It doesn't stop my mind from being active,' he said, 'and when I go home at night I can still immerse myself in the few books I have left.' We sat down with him under his canvas canopy and munched away happily while he told us stories from the Bhagavad Gita, which he had read and reread and which he said was the greatest book ever written. Some of the ideas he talked about were so complex that I couldn't understand them, and I knew that Sandeep didn't even try, but I enjoyed listening, and while I listened I enjoyed looking out from our shady perch and watching the passers-by.

When it was time for Bharat to close down for the night, we helped him clean his griddle and put away his utensils. At least that made us feel as if we had earned our puris. Bharat always said the same thing, though, when we said our goodbyes. 'You should go home. The streets are no place for young children.'

He knew what my reply would be. I had told him the very first time he had said it. 'We can't go home. Our father doesn't want us there.'

'What about your mother?'

'It's better for our mother when we're not there,' I insisted.

'A mother dies inside without her children.'

'Our mother was suffering because of us.'

'Have you written to tell her you're all right?'

'I will,' I replied. 'I will soon.'

I kept putting it off, though. I didn't want to

write to her until I had a good job and could send money home. I didn't want her to know that my brother and I were ragpickers. I wanted to be able to tell her something that would make her proud and stop her from worrying. What mother would want to be told that her children scavenged through the leftovers dumped outside expensive restaurants to feed their starving bellies? And what mother would want to learn that her children's clothes were infested with fleas, their skin burnt and sore, their feet bare and scarred? It hadn't taken very long for us to look like all the other street children. But at least in looking like them we felt more as if we belonged.

The cricket helped even more. We met every Sunday afternoon, lots of us. It was one of the highlights of the week to go to the building site after work and hit a ball around. We discovered that once every two months, the ragpickers' team played a match against one of the other groups of children: the shoe-shine boys or the water-sellers, the garland-makers or the errand runners. The ragpickers were due to play a match against the garland-makers five weeks after we arrived. We practised together, not just the ragpickers but the other groups as well, but when it came to choosing who was going to play in the match, Vikas, who seemed to be in charge of all the arrangements, kept our team a big secret right until the last minute. He called us to gather round him and, when he was sure that none of the other teams could overhear, told us who would be batting and who would be bowling. In another corner, the captain of the garland-makers was doing the same thing. Arun pranced round the outside of our huddle, threatening to give away our secrets if we didn't let him play for us. Vikas told us to ignore him because he did the same thing before every match. It was the only time that being a ragpicker – or any of the other street trades – had any appeal for him. He wanted so much to play for one of the teams, but they were united in not letting him in.

Vikas picked me for that first match and promised Sandeep that he would have his chance in the next. Sandeep wasn't very happy. He accepted Vikas's decision, but grumbled to me when we were alone on our island. On the day of the match, he said he wouldn't come and watch.

'Don't be such a bad sport,' I said. 'We need you to support us. Anyway, I'm not leaving you on your own.'

'You can't always make me stay with you,' he challenged.

I glared at him. 'No. I can't make you, not if you're stupid enough to think that you'll be all right on your own.'

'We've been here long enough now,' he argued. 'It's not as if I'm going to get lost.'

'Why don't you want to come to the match?' I asked. 'Don't you want to cheer our team on? Don't you want us to win?'

'Don't care,' he said sullenly.

When it was time to go, he trailed along behind me. I was sure that once he was with the other ragpickers who hadn't been chosen for the team, he would soon join in. I was so nervous about playing, I didn't really want to have to worry about my brother as well. There had been a lot of banter amongst all the street children about how the flower boys had beaten the ragpickers when they had played on the previous occasion, and how the ragpickers would not want to lose to the flower boys again. Arun, in particular, had wound things up, saying that he was going to support the team that smelt the sweetest. He seemed to have more of a grudge against Vikas for not letting him play than he did against the captain of the other team.

191

I was amazed at how many kids, and a few adults, poured through the gap in the fence as we warmed up. There was an air of huge excitement. I hadn't expected that. This was a major event in the lives of the street dwellers and they all wanted to be part of it. They crowded round us and patted us on the back before finding themselves a place to sit round the edge. I felt as if I were about to step out for the Indian team against Australia or Pakistan or England. It was a terrifying feeling, but it was exhilarating as well. A great cheer went up when Vikas and the other captain tossed a coin to decide who would bat first. I prayed it wouldn't be us. I wanted to start off in the field to get used to being there, though I was petrified that I might drop a catch in front of all those people.

We lost the toss. The garland-makers chose to bat. Vikas gave us our fielding positions and I made my way to third slip. Sandeep sat himself down just behind the boundary, which we had marked out with pieces of rubble. Arun had arrived and was talking to the opening batsmen for the opposition. Then, when they set off towards the wicket, I watched him seek out my brother. He sat down next to him and Sandeep was soon creased up with laughter. I wondered what was so funny, but the match was starting and I needed to concentrate.

The opening batsmen were very strong and hit fifteen off our first two overs. Every run was greeted with wild cheering from one half of the crowd and loud boos from the other, though it was all in good humour. I soon noticed that Sandeep was copying Arun and cheering for the garland-makers. I tried to swallow my annoyance. He only wanted to make himself look big, I reasoned, and at least he was sitting with someone I knew. Vikas shouted at me to move back a bit. Chintu had replaced the previous bowler, Ashok, who had had twenty-two runs taken off him in only three overs. I bent down ready as Chintu ran in and bowled a medium-paced ball with plenty of spin. The ball swung in at the last minute, the batsman was slightly off balance when he struck it, and it soared high into the air. Tej, at second slip, and I charged off in the direction we thought it would come down. I was the quickest. Squinting against the sun, I watched as it reached its peak, then followed its line as it began to drop. I could feel my nerves jangling, threatening my hands with their fear. But I took that catch. I took it and held it and heard every ragpicker in that makeshift ground erupt with joy. As the other members of the team skipped over to pat me on the back, I looked to see if Sandeep was cheering. He wasn't there. Neither was Arun. I scoured the rows of supporters, but couldn't see them anywhere.

Chapter 19

I couldn't concentrate once I was aware that Sandeep had disappeared. I was torn between playing for my team and looking for him. The remainder of the garland-makers' innings went by in a blur. Chintu took two more quick wickets, and Vikas took three, but it didn't stop our opponents from building a very large total. As soon as we had bowled our final over and before we went out to bat, I grabbed the chance to walk round the boundary to see if I could spot my brother.

I was halfway round, when a sudden commotion by the gap in the fence caused everyone to fall quiet, to crane their necks to see what was happening, then to leap to their feet. A figure flashed across the centre of the cricket pitch, followed by at least half a dozen policemen.

It was Arun.

The minute they realised he was one of us, the street dwellers closed ranks. Without making it obvious, they obstructed the path of the policemen by blundering around, seemingly panic-stricken. I *was* panic-stricken. Where was Sandeep? I couldn't see anything clearly any more. I was being jostled by the crowd, first one way, then the other. I struggled to keep my feet on the ground. I twisted and ducked to avoid flailing arms. Shouts of encouragement were punched into the air. 'Go on, Arun. Keep going, Arun.'

A rift suddenly appeared through the army of bodies surrounding me. I heard the great gasps for breath first, then saw the whites of his eyes as he hurtled past me. The rift closed immediately behind him. The thundering of the policemen's feet was brought to a halt. 'Get out of our way, scum,' I heard. 'You'll be sorry for this.' There were screams when they got out their truncheons and brought them down on the heads of anyone who blocked their path. The boy in front of me fell to the ground, blood seeping from a wound above his eye. To my horror I saw that it was Chintu. The police barged their way through, not caring that they trampled on his body. I felt sick. I wanted to run away but there was nowhere to run. The crowd had closed again behind the policemen. They were surging forward to see what would happen next. Then a cheer rang out and somebody said that Arun had made it through the gap in the fence, and that the distance between him and the police was getting bigger all the time.

Everywhere groups of boys were chattering excitedly, some of them bragging about how they had thwarted the police. The fear had gone from their eyes and they began betting whether or not Arun would get away this time. Most of them were sure he would. Some thought his luck might have run out. Chintu was on his feet, holding a dirty rag to his temple and clutching his thigh. Tej was by his side, his hand holding on to Chintu's elbow, his face tight with shock.

'Are you all right?' I asked anxiously. At the same time I scoured the crowd for some sign of Sandeep.

'I would have preferred those policemen not to be wearing boots,' Chintu grinned, before wincing with pain. 'I hope he got away.'

'Who cares whether he got away,' I said angrily. 'If he was up to no good, it's his own fault if he gets caught. And it's because of him I don't know where my brother is.'

Chintu stared at me in astonishment and was about to speak when Vikas found us.

'Cricket's off,' he announced. 'If the police don't catch Arun, they might want to make scapegoats of the rest of us.'

'Have you seen Sandeep?' Chintu took the words from my mouth.

'Not since the beginning of the match,' Vikas replied. 'He was with Arun.'

'Well, he's not now,' I cried, 'and I don't know where he is or if he's in trouble. I need to find him.'

'We'll help you,' said Chintu immediately.

'No you won't,' said Vikas. 'You need to look after that cut. The rest of us will search. Let's hope he wasn't involved in whatever it was Arun was up to.'

Vikas rounded up several of the other ragpickers and we all set off in different directions. I decided to go back to our island first. I thought that was where I was most likely to find Sandeep. I hurried through the streets, which were packed with families enjoying their Sunday walks. There was no sign of him anywhere. I wished we could be with my mother and father, strolling along happily like everyone else, but that was a wish that would never come true. Our family didn't exist any more.

When I reached our island, he wasn't there. A policeman was directing traffic close by. I hid in the shadows of a doorway, wondering whether I should wait there for Sandeep to return, or try somewhere else. Where, though? The only place I could think of was the roof by the tannery, but I imagined that Vikas would look there first. I decided to head in that direction anyway. If Vikas had found him, he would surely tell him to wait there for me.

I heard voices as I approached the tannery. I climbed up to the roof, ready to lash Sandeep with my tongue. I was met by a group of five boys, who had jumped to their feet ready to pounce on any intruder. They visibly relaxed when they saw it was nobody of any importance. They staggered back to a corner and resumed their smoking.

Not before I recognised the one who had stolen my shoes. He was still wearing them, oblivious of the fact that I was their owner. My pulse began to race. I'd let him get away last time. Was I going to let him get away again?

'You got a problem?' one of the boys asked when he saw that I was still standing there.

'He's after one of our joints,' the boy wearing my shoes sniggered.

'I'm after my shoes,' I said firmly.

'Who's got your shoes?' another boy asked.

'He has.' I pointed.

'You wanna be careful making accusations like that.' The boy who was wearing my shoes stood up and walked towards me. 'You could upset somebody a lot making accusations like that – specially if they're not true.'

'They're my shoes and you know it.'

The other four boys stood up and walked towards me.

I held my ground for as long as I could. 'You'll be sorry,' I threatened.

'Not half as sorry as you will be,' said the boy I had accused. He lunged towards me.

I fled. Bravery was one thing, but one against five was stupidity. He could have my shoes. I wasn't going to wait there to see what would happen. I ran to Bharat Gupta's stall to see if Sandeep had gone there. The old man hadn't seen him, but told me not to worry and that he would turn up.

'Your brother has a mind of his own and sometimes it will get him into trouble, but I believe he can look after himself,' he said.

I wanted to tell him about the glue-sniffing. I wanted to tell him how difficult it was to look after my brother when I was just a boy myself. I wanted to tell him I was afraid Sandeep would fall under the influence of the wrong people and how I hated it that he thought so much of Arun.

'Stay here and your brother will come looking for you,' he advised.

'But what if the police have got him?'

'Then I will make some enquiries.'

I wished I could stay with Bharat, but how could I when my friends were all out searching? 'I can't just sit here,' I said.

Bharat patted me on the arm. 'If he comes by, I'll tie him to my stall,' he promised.

I set off again. I had one last thought about where I might find Sandeep if he was in trouble. On the wasteland by the slums. He could blend in with the slum dwellers there. I walked as fast as I could, cursing my brother for the worry he was causing me, especially if it was because he had been doing something he shouldn't. Arun was behind his disappearance, I was sure, but that didn't excuse Sandeep.

I reached the street that led on to the wasteland and ran down it. I had made myself believe that as soon as I reached the end I would see my brother sitting on one of the boulders waiting for me. I'm surprised that I didn't imagine him lit up by the remaining rays of sunshine, Bollywood-poster style.

He wasn't there.

I looked all around, even on the tip, but there was no sign of him. I sat down on a boulder myself, exhausted, and tried to decide what to do next. It was possible that one of the other boys had found Sandeep and gone back to our island with him. If they had, I hoped they would wait there for me. And if Sandeep had gone back on his own, I hoped he would stay there too. It was time for me to stop running around after him and let him come to me. I sat there for a few minutes longer, summoning the energy to go back, while I watched the slum dwellers carrying their spoils down from the tip. I checked them one by one to make sure my brother wasn't amongst them. As I did, I saw Vikas's familiar figure scrambling down the slope.

I was so surprised that I sat with my mouth

gaping, until my surprise turned to indignation. He was supposed to be searching for my brother, not digging around on a rubbish tip. He was supposed to be our friend. I stood up to go. I didn't want to talk to him.

It was too late. He had seen me and was waving at me to wait for him. I hesitated. I needed to know why he wasn't searching. I wanted an explanation.

He crossed the railway line, pushed through the hedge and ran across the wasteground towards me. 'Have you found him?' he panted.

'No,' I said coldly.

'They caught Arun,' he said. 'He's in big trouble this time. He stole some jewellery.'

'Was Sandeep with him?' My voice was little more than a whisper.

'Not when Arun was arrested.' Vikas fixed me with a stare. 'I looked everywhere for him,' he said shortly. 'So did the others. We couldn't find him. The police haven't got him but, according to Meera, two boys were involved in the robbery and someone identified Arun.'

'Did anyone know who the other boy was?' I hardly dared ask.

'He was off before anyone could get a good look at

him. If it was Sandeep, then he got away this time and he'll come out of hiding once he thinks it's safe. But he'd better not try anything like that again.'

'It couldn't have been Sandeep,' I said defensively. 'He wouldn't do anything like that.'

Vikas put his hand on my shoulder. 'We all do stupid things when we're desperate, and then we learn not to do them again.'

'But he wasn't desperate,' I protested. 'We've stopped being desperate.'

'Unhappy, then,' said Vikas.

'If he did anything like that it's because Arun made him. It's all Arun's fault.' I pulled away from Vikas and started to march towards the street that led back into the city. I expected him to come after me – I wanted him to come after me – but when I turned he was walking over to one of the rocks. He doesn't care, I thought angrily to myself. He just cares about himself and collecting his stupid rubbish.

I started to run, pounding my feet on the ground, not bothering where I was treading, wanting to hurt myself to feed my anger further. If people got in my way, I barged past them, ignoring their protests and words of contempt. Why should I feel anything but contempt for them too, when in their eyes I shouldn't exist? I resented their happy lives when my own had turned so sour. I was reduced to collecting rubbish. My brother was reduced to stealing. How much lower could you get? And I'd admitted it, in my heart: I knew it was my brother who had been involved in the robbery. It was all my father's fault. If he hadn't lost his job, if he hadn't started drinking, if he hadn't started beating my mother, beating me, if he hadn't abandoned his responsibility as a father and left me to pick up the pieces, then none of this would have happened. I didn't ask for it and I didn't want it. For all his fine words about the importance of school and a good job, he had been the one to tear them away from us and leave us with no hope for the future. How I hated him.

Chapter 20

I was still in a fury when I got back to our island. Sandeep wasn't there. The light was beginning to fade and the streets were emptying. I kicked my way over to our rubble hideout, sat down and waited. There was nothing else I could do. As I waited, my fears began to suppress everything else I was feeling. I was afraid for Sandeep, not just that day but for every day we were living on the streets. He had a stubbornness about him. He was too easily influenced and attracted to the wrong people. He was only nine and easy prey for someone like Arun. I had become the voice of authority as far as Sandeep was concerned, and he didn't like my telling him what to do, even if he knew I was right. If only he'd understand that I didn't like it either. If only he could see that I didn't like having to turn adult overnight, that I wanted to go back to being a boy at school learning my lessons so that one day I would have a good job. That I wanted to go back to being a boy in our village, with a mother and father and friends and having fun. I was afraid for myself as well as for Sandeep.

I sat legs crossed, head bowed, rocking occasionally. Little by little, the darkness grew around me, and still I sat there. It was only when a car horn blared that I was startled into action. I stood up and looked around. I was completely alone. The streets nearby were deserted and for a brief moment there was no traffic. It didn't last. A rickshaw trundled by in the middle of the road, followed by a truck that was anxious to overtake it. I saw the rickshaw-wallah's face. He was smiling, happy to enjoy his few seconds of power over the bully behind him before he was forced to give way.

I had no idea what time it was by then, but I decided to go back over to our island. I pulled our bags from their rubble hiding-place. As I did so, I heard the tinkle of metal. I assumed I had disturbed an old nail, but bent down to find it because one of the ragpickers would be grateful for it. I felt around in the dark. My fingers touched something that clinked as it moved. It was a metal chain. I picked it up and carried it to the light of a street lamp. In the dull glow I could see that the chain was gold.

The minute I realised what it was I shoved it in my pocket. I didn't want to hold it. It was like holding something poisonous. I knew now what my brother had done. I had hoped he might be innocent. He wasn't. The evidence was already burning its way through my shorts. What was I supposed to do with it? And then I saw a police car driving slowly up the road. I was standing right in the headlights, caught red-handed. I watched as the car approached me. I was unable to move. Then, when I thought it was going to stop, I ran. I dived down a side street, along an alley-way, and kept going. I had to put as much distance as I could between the policeman and myself. I came to a tall apartment block with parking spaces to one side. I ran round the back of it and in through the door, which opened on to some stairs. I climbed the first flight then leant against a wall while I tried to catch my breath.

That was all I could hear. My breathing. It sounded so loud, I expected somebody to come out of one of the apartments and ask me what I was up to. When I was calmer, my breathing under control, I could hear a television. I imagined that on the other side of the wall of the nearest apartment, someone was sitting on a comfortable chair watching a film. I listened for a moment, trying to work out what the voices were saying. I couldn't make anything out above the background music, but I could imagine the beautiful women, the handsome men, the colourful costumes and the stunning scenery. I'd seen them so often on the huge advertising boards all over the city, and on the rows of television screens in department-store windows. I took the gold necklace from my pocket and placed it on the doorstep of the apartment. It belonged there more than it did with me, and nothing in this world would have made me keep it. I walked back out on to the street, checked that there was no sign of the police car, and made my way cautiously in the direction of our island.

The island was still unoccupied when I reached it. I wasn't surprised. I wouldn't have expected Sandeep to be sitting there on his own. I turned then towards our hideout. He was there, hidden in the shadows but I could see him. He had his back to me and was digging in the rubble. I couldn't help feeling relieved, but I was angry, so angry. I walked over to him. He was so busy digging that he didn't even hear me.

'I've thrown it away,' I said.

He spun round. 'Thrown what away?' he said sharply. He wouldn't look me in the eye.

'The necklace you stole.'

'I didn't steal anything,' he protested.

'Don't lie to me, Sandeep,' I hissed. 'Where have you been? I've been going out of my head with worry.'

'I told you before, I can look after myself.'

'No you can't. You can't look after yourself at all. The minute I'm not there you get into trouble.'

'I'm not in trouble.' He scowled at me defiantly.

'Only because you got lucky. Do you realise what would have happened if the police had found the necklace on you?'

'That wasn't my fault,' Sandeep replied sulkily. 'Arun made me go with him. I didn't know what he was going to do.'

'Arun didn't make you do anything,' I countered. 'If you can look after yourself then you can say no to someone like Arun.'

'At least he doesn't nag me all the time. At least I can have fun with him.'

'You nearly landed up in prison because of him!' I was shouting now. I couldn't believe I was being compared with Arun and coming off worse.

We stood in silence. Sandeep still wouldn't look at me. He shifted uncomfortably. His feet were covered in cuts, some of them bleeding. His hair was matted and dull. He sat down and his shoulders began to shake. He sniffed loudly and wiped his arm across his nose. Then he began to sob. I sat down next to him and waited for him to speak. I wasn't prepared to comfort him. He didn't deserve that.

At last, he muttered, 'He said we were just going to have a look.'

'Have a look at what?'

'The shops. He said if they wouldn't let him play in the cricket then he didn't see why he should sit around and watch it. So I said that they wouldn't let me play either and I didn't see why I should watch it. He said he would take me to the shops instead and show me how to persuade people to give me things. He promised to show me how I would never have to be a ragpicker again and said he could get me the best meal I'd ever had if I went with him. So I did, because I was hungry and I'm fed up with always being hungry, even if it is better than it was, and I'm fed up with being a ragpicker because it's the most horrible job in the world.'

'It's better than begging,' I interjected, 'and it's

better than stealing. At least we're doing something important.'

'Who says it's important? That's just what you say because it makes you feel better about it. If it's so important, then why do people treat us as if we're scum?'

'Not everyone does,' I said.

'Most people do and you know it. Anyway, I went with him and we went to a few shops and he always came out with something he'd taken but I never saw him do it. He said he would show me how and that we could work as a team because I could be a lookout for him.'

'So you said, "Yes, O mighty Arun, I will do that for you."'

'No I didn't, what do you take me for?' he protested. 'I said it was wrong to steal things and he laughed. He said it was wrong that everybody else had everything they wanted and we didn't have anything. We were outside a jeweller's shop then. He told me to wait at the door while he went in to look for a necklace for his mother. He said they might be suspicious if we both went in, and he didn't want them thinking he was up to no good when he wasn't. The next thing I knew, he'd grabbed a necklace from a stand and was pushing past me into the street. He told me to run if I didn't want to get into trouble, so I ran after him. There must have been police close by because they were after us in no time. Then, when we went round a corner, Arun threw the necklace to me and told me to go in a different direction. "It's your present from me," he said, and that was the last I saw of him.'

'He wanted you to get caught with it instead of him,' I said angrily.

'No he didn't,' Sandeep argued. 'He wanted me to keep it because he likes me.'

'Well, it's gone now, and you're lucky the police didn't catch you.'

'I was too clever,' Sandeep mumbled smugly. Before I could tell him off, he started sobbing again, telling me how frightened he had been every time the police were close to finding him. I couldn't work out whether he was crying just to make me feel sorry for him, or whether he was genuinely shocked and upset. I decided to wait until he was calm again before I said anything else. I wanted him to understand how much pain he had caused me; how by going with Arun he had not only put himself in danger of landing up in a police cell, but had ruined the day for the rest of us; how he kept letting me down.

It was Sandeep who spoke next, and what he said stunned me.

'Why did you throw the necklace away? We could have sold it and bought things with what we got. We could have bought food for the next six months. We could have bought new clothes, shoes, something better to sleep on. What did you have to go and throw it away for?'

I stood up. 'Are you completely stupid?' I hurled at him. 'Have you forgotten everything our mother taught us?' I began to walk away from him towards our island.

'It doesn't count here,' he shouted after me. 'It's different. We're trying to survive here. It's easy to be good when someone puts food in front of you every day and you've got somewhere decent to live. And I didn't steal the necklace, Arun did.'

I turned and fired back, 'It doesn't mean we have to throw away the values we've been taught along with the rest of the city's rubbish.'

I closed my ears to his reply. I didn't want to hear any more. I was scared of what my brother was becoming. I felt useless, too. I didn't seem to be able to stop what was happening. I sat down on the island and stared out at the empty streets. Perhaps it was time for us to go home. Perhaps if we did, things would be better. Appa might have got himself a new job. He might be longing for us to go back so that he could tell us all about it. We could play cricket with him again with the rest of the boys in the village. The pain I felt at not being able to be with Amma was excruciating. I wanted to help her crush spices in the kitchen. I wanted to walk to the village shop with her. I wanted to have her fuss round me because a button on my shirt was undone or my shoes were scuffed. I wanted to go to sleep with her goodnight kiss wet on my cheek.

Sandeep came and sat beside me. 'I'm sorry, Suresh,' he whispered.

I couldn't answer.

'Arun makes it sound as if it's all right,' he continued.

'It's not all right,' I murmured. 'If it was all right he wouldn't be in prison now.'

'Will they let him out? They won't hurt him, will they?'

I felt like saying that I didn't care, but, despite what Arun had done, he was one of us. 'I don't know, Sandeep. I don't think we'll see him for a while.'

'He only did it because he didn't have anything to eat and because he wanted to play in the cricket.'

'He should work, then, like the rest of us.'

'It's horrible work. I hate it.'

He leaned his head against my arm. I stiffened at first, but relented and put my arm round his shoulder. 'Is Vikas very angry with me?' he asked.

'Do you care?'

He nodded. 'I promise I won't do it again,' he said.

We both sat there with our thoughts for a while, then my brother said quietly, 'When can we go home, Suresh? I want to go home.'

I didn't answer straight away. Then I said, gently, 'This is our home now. If we work even harder and save up some money, we'll be able to make an even better home. But we'll write to Amma soon and if she tells us that Appa is well again, then perhaps we can go back to see them.'

'And if Appa is well, we'll stay won't we?'

I nodded my head. 'If Appa is well, then we'll stay.'

Chapter 21

The city was smothered in dust, everything was so dry. People stayed under cover as much as possible, diving into air-conditioned shops or seeking out overhanging roofs for shelter. You could almost see the thousands of tongues hanging out, desperate to catch the first drops of rain when they fell. The water level in the canal dropped rapidly. What was left was fetid and thick with waste. There was no shelter on the bank either, unless you arrived early and found a spot under the bridge. We washed the glass as best we could, leaning over the edge of the canal and brushing it to and fro amongst the reeds. While we did, the sun beat down on us, burning our arms and legs. It became so bad and there was so little water remaining, that eventually we had to abandon the canal altogether and find somewhere else. There was nowhere on our morning route, which meant that we had to go right out of our way to wash our pickings before returning to hand them over to Mr Roy.

I wondered how we would ever save any money. Mr Roy continued to pay us as little as possible, reducing what we thought we were due because of a hole in my sack, a drop in the value of glass, and anything else he could dream up. Vikas told us to expect less and then we wouldn't be disappointed. I did always expect less, but I was still disappointed. I thought that if we stayed with the job, Mr Roy would reward us for our loyalty, but he continued to treat us with suspicion, as if he expected us to walk away at any moment.

'He trusts you,' I said to Vikas. 'Why won't he trust us?'

'Because it will cost him more to trust you,' Vikas replied. 'He only keeps me sweet because he might need my help one day.'

Word went round that the police were going to make an example of Arun and keep him imprisoned for at least a year, even though he was only sixteen. Sandeep was shocked when he heard the news. I think he believed that Arun would be back on the streets in two or three days. At least, I told myself, my brother

218

will think twice about stealing again. The whole community of street dwellers was upset by the news. Arun, for all his arrogance, was a popular figure. He made them laugh with tales of his brushes with authority, and they admired his bravado. I was secretly glad that he was no longer there to lead Sandeep astray.

We continued to play cricket, but the team captains decided to abandon all further matches until any unrest between the police and the street dwellers had died down. Nobody wanted to risk a full-on confrontation. I was disappointed, and Sandeep grumbled that he hadn't had a chance to play. He shut up, though, as soon as he saw the look I gave him.

Our best times continued to be the nights we spent on the roof next to the tannery. They allowed us to forget about the daily difficulties we faced, especially when the heat became so suffocating that we had to stop working earlier and accept even smaller payouts from our dealers. Chintu developed a series of playlets based upon the interaction between the police, the gods and a group of burglars. At every performance he added a new sequence and involved one or more of his audience. Tej accompanied him on his devil chaser, while others of us joined in by drumming on barrels, beating pieces of wood together, tapping on pipes, and whistling through our teeth. The laughter and music kept us going.

Just when it seemed as if the earth would crack into hundreds of pieces and taps would spurt out nothing but dust, it started to rain. A few drops fell early one morning and woke us up. We lay on our backs looking up at the sky with our mouths open, catching the drops of naked rain that strayed our way and giggling foolishly. Amma had always told us to bathe ourselves in the first rains of the season to prevent or relieve heat sores. Sandeep and I were both covered in them. By the time we set off for work, it was raining harder and thick black clouds blocked out the sun. Nothing could dampen our spirits though, nor those of the townspeople who had ventured out early on hearing the rain spattering on their roofs. Everyone wore a smile, even for us.

Vikas was less enthusiastic. 'A bit of rain's all right,' he said, 'but the monsoon makes our job more difficult.'

We didn't let that stop us from scampering over mounds of rubbish and digging through overflowing bins with renewed energy.

When we lived in our village, the coming of the monsoon was always greeted with cries of joy, like the birth of a long-awaited first child. By the time it arrived, the farmers were desperate for rain to revive their parched fields and save their crops and animals. The first drops sent up puffs of dust that gradually joined together in red-tinged clouds as the sky closed in. I remembered the exotic smell of damp earth, and the calls of the peacocks who saw it as the perfect time to court their hens. All the villagers gathered under the neem tree and chattered excitedly about the new season. There was an air of festivity, which led to celebratory feasts of pakora and spiced tea in every house. We were looking forward to being part of the city when it began its own celebrations.

By the middle of the day it was dry again. The sky was clear and the sun beat down, wiping out every last shred of evidence that the rain had broken through. Still nobody talked about anything except the impending monsoon.

'The city could do with a good clean,' Vikas observed when we sat down with a group of friends to eat our lunch.

'So could our feet,' Chintu laughed.

As one we gazed down at our feet. The dirt was so ingrained, especially in the cracked edges, I doubted that even a month of monsoon rains would wash them clean.

A large rat ran along the path in front of us. It stopped briefly, looked at us, licked its paws, then darted off round a corner.

'See, even the rat agrees,' Chintu grinned.

'I bet Arun will be glad he's inside when the monsoon starts,' said Sandeep.

'I bet he won't,' argued Vikas. 'It'll be boiling hot and there'll be no air and everybody will be on top of each other. I've seen it for myself. No one would want to be in there. Not any time.'

'Poor Arun,' said Chintu.

Tej nodded his head in agreement. Vikas's face was expressionless. I was happy enough with my own life at that moment to feel sorry for Arun too.

Chapter 22

When I woke the next morning, the sky was pitch-black. I had no idea what time it was. I guessed by the amount of traffic going by that we should be getting up, but it was so dark that it felt like the middle of the night. The monsoon clouds had gathered ominously and were waiting to dump their load on us. A rickshaw scurried by and its owner cried out gleefully, 'She is coming. See? The monsoon is coming. When it comes I will do big business.' Another rickshaw-wallah waved and called out, 'Hey, you on your island, a big wave is coming to wash you away.' He laughed, rang his bell excitedly and continued his haphazard course.

The air hung heavy and humid as my brother and I trekked across the city to begin our work. Daylight broke through in patches, but the black clouds were thick and threatening. By midmorning the atmosphere had become so oppressive that something had to give. A few large drops fell to the ground by my feet. I looked up, half expecting a monkey to be bombarding me with nutshells. It wasn't long before the drops were tumbling faster and faster.

In less than an hour we were soaked through. The rain was coming down in torrents. The more it rained, the happier everyone became. Now there was a carnival atmosphere in the streets. Young and old cavorted wildly, running along, splashing in puddles, spinning in circles to make sure every last inch of their bodies and clothes was dripping wet. When down-pipes began to overflow, we stood under them to enjoy an open-air shower. The weight of the rain made canopies bend over street traders' stalls. Every so often their owners stood and beat them upwards, sending water cascading over passers-by. Nobody minded, so great was everyone's delight in being cool for a moment. The only thing that spoilt it for us was when Mr Roy complained about our soaking wet sacks and docked our wages because we made his floor dirty, which meant that he would have to pay some-body to clean it.

The rain continued all day long. On the way home in the late afternoon, we stopped to talk with Bharat.

He was dry under his canopy, which nevertheless sagged threateningly over his griddle.

'Our prayers have been answered,' he said, 'and just in time. The gods know how to make us sweat before they give us what we want.'

'It hasn't stopped all day,' said Sandeep, sticking his foot out to block a stream of water that was running down the road.

'Nor will it stop for many days,' observed Bharat. 'So my fortune-teller friend tells me, and he should know, though it doesn't take a fortune teller to realise that the monsoon has finally arrived.' He nodded to a man who was sitting on a stool to his left. The man was unprotected by the canopy and his long hair and grizzly beard dripped continuously.

'Tell your fortunes,' he said to us, as though he had suddenly been prompted to perform.

I shook my head. 'No money,' I explained.

'Your luck is round the corner,' the man offered, smiling toothlessly.

'I'm going to be a leader,' Sandeep told him.

'Not until you have served your time as a follower,' the man warned.

Sandeep shrugged his shoulders and kicked at a pool of water. Bharat grinned at me.

'This is a day to share puris with friends,' he announced. He put some dough on to the griddle and we watched hungrily as it bubbled and ballooned. Having earned so little that day, we were grateful for this treat. He scraped them up one by one, put them on to pieces of paper and handed them to us. 'Let us hope for enough rain to fill our rivers and canals and wash our city clean,' he said.

'Be careful with your wishes,' the fortune teller warned. 'You will not want to offend the sun god.'

'No offence intended,' said Bharat, 'but I am happy for Surya to rest for a few days and let Indra take over.'

'Days are nothing in the passing of a year,' the fortune teller replied. 'It is only when they turn to weeks that they gain importance.'

'Pah! Every day is important,' retorted Bharat. 'You are full of nonsense, my friend. And I am not asking for Surya to rest for weeks.'

Sandeep and I looked at each other in amusement, wondering what the two men were talking about. All I knew was that we needed rain. We continued to sit with Bharat and the fortune teller for the rest of the afternoon. It was fun listening to the rain beating down all around us and watching people splash their way through the increasingly deep puddles that had formed in the potholed pavements and roads. It was good to feel that we were being included when Bharat's regular customers stopped by to drink chai and chat with him. Because everybody looked bedraggled, we no longer stood out as street dwellers. We were just kids enjoying the first rain that had fallen on the city for nine long months. When, finally, Bharat closed his shop, an hour later than usual, Sandeep and I set off back to our island, arm-in-arm and with a great sense of belonging to this city.

It was the last night we spent on our island. By the time we moved over to it from our rubble waiting-station, the rain had slowed to a drizzle, but what little grass there was left was soaking wet and pitted with pools of water. Bharat had lent us some plastic sheeting, which we laid on the ground and wrapped round ourselves. It wasn't very comfortable. It stuck to our legs and the wet crept in round the edges. Whenever a big truck trundled past, showers of water splashed over us, leaving us wetter than ever.

'If the monsoon goes on for too long, our island might disappear altogether,' Sandeep giggled.

'We might find ourselves floating away down the road,' I joined in.

'Where do you think we'll end up?' Sandeep asked. 'In the canal?'

'In the slums,' I laughed.

'Not me,' proclaimed Sandeep. 'I'd rather be washed completely away.'

We both knew it was not really something to laugh about, and I was trying to think where we might go to keep dry. I hoped that somebody might allow us to squeeze in next to them under an overhanging roof or in a covered doorway. I was sure that Vikas would help us, or Chintu. I fell asleep, at last, comforted by the thought that we had friends who would know what to do.

We were woken when a truck rolled by and sent a tidal wave of water over us. The rain was so torrential, I couldn't believe we'd slept through it. Everywhere was in darkness. Even the street lamps were out.

'There must be a power cut,' I said to Sandeep.

'I can't see a thing,' he replied.

Another truck rumbled down the road, lighting us up briefly before drowning us. A dog barked somewhere close by. I heard a scuffling noise behind me. I tried to force my eyes to see but I couldn't tell if the black shapes that seemed to be moving round the edges of the island were real or my mind playing tricks.

'What's that over there?' I asked Sandeep, pointing.

'Where?'

'To my right.'

'I can't see which way you're facing.'

A loud moo made my heart boomerang across my chest. The black shape I was looking at was a cow.

'It's a cow,' Sandeep laughed.

'Clever,' I said.

'Do you think it's lost?' Sandeep laughed again.

'What time do you think it is?'

'Whatever time it is, I'm not going to work in this dark.'

'We're going to have to move,' I said. 'We can't stay here, it's too wet.'

We both fell silent as a taxi and a rickshaw went past, fixing us in their headlights, frightening away the cow, abandoning us to the darkness again.

'I wish we didn't have to move,' muttered Sandeep.

'So do I,' I replied, 'but we'll catch pneumonia if we stay here. We need to find somewhere dry. We can always move back after the monsoon.'

'If somebody doesn't take it from us.'

'We might find somewhere better,' I said optimistically.

I guessed that it must be close to the time when we would normally set off for work, judging by the numbers of trucks going by and the buses carrying factory workers. We sat there wrapped in our sodden blankets and plastic sheeting, waiting for daylight to penetrate the monsoon clouds, or for the city's power supply to function again. Gradually, oil lamps began to flicker inside houses as people woke to discover that they had no electricity.

And then, just like that, the lights went on again. Off. Then on again.

'It's like someone's playing with the switches,' said Sandeep.

'It's the monsoon playing with the wires,' I said. 'Come on, it's time we got going.'

We dumped our things amongst the rubble and set off across the city. It was as if everyone had been waiting for the lights to go on because the streets were suddenly swarming with rickshaws and taxis. We were so wet already that it didn't matter that we were splashed whenever one went by. In fact, we went out of our way to get drenched because it protected us against the humidity that was unleashed as the rain lashed the hot earth. It didn't take long for the traffic to come to a complete standstill, the numbers of vehicles swollen because of the weather. The cacophony of horns and bells and hooters was accompanied by a chorus of braying and mooing from donkeys and oxen that were caught in the chaos. The smiles were still there, though, not just on the faces of the rickshaw-wallahs and taxi drivers who were 'doing big business', but on those of their passengers who were enjoying a novel means of getting to work and chattering ani-matedly through the windows of their chosen mode of transport.

Our own work wasn't much fun that day. It wouldn't get any better, either, Vikas warned us. He had shaved his head since he saw us last, because he was fed up with his hair dripping into his eyes, and it would also be one less place for the fleas to hide. 'If you think this is bad,' he said, when Sandeep complained having put his hands through a glutinous mess of newspaper, curry and banana skins, 'you wait till it's been raining for several days and nobody's done anything to clear the old stuff.' Some of the rubbish was being washed down the roads and into the overflow channels that were supposed to carry away excess water. Several drains were already blocked with plastic bags and cardboard, causing rising pools of water around them.

It had all seemed like a game when we first set off, leaping through puddles, kicking water at each other and dancing under gutters. By the middle of the morning the game had turned sour and I couldn't wait for the day to end. At least the glass we collected didn't weigh more wet than it did dry, but our sacks certainly did and they rubbed our shoulders raw. All the time, at the back of my mind, though I had tried to ignore it, was the knowledge that we had nowhere to sleep that night.

When we arrived at Mr Roy's, he told us that because he would have to pay extra to transport his recycled goods through the monsoon, he would have to pay us less.

'By the time I've paid for the extra hours it'll take, there'll be precious little left,' he said. 'And I'm not a charity.'

I don't know what happened then. All of a sudden, everything just blew inside my head without any warning. I thought I was all right. I thought I was used to the bad things that kept happening. I thought I was used to Mr Roy and his tricks. But I wasn't. I couldn't just stand there in my sopping wet clothes and listen to him going on about how difficult life was for him. I lost my temper.

'What do you mean life's difficult for you?' I shouted. 'Your life's not difficult. You just sit around while your army of slaves does all your dirty work. And then you don't even pay us what you owe us.'

'You'd better tell your friend to shut it or I won't pay him at all,' he said to Vikas. 'I always knew he was trouble that one.'

'Better do as Mr Roy says,' Vikas warned me.

'Why should I do what he says when he doesn't play fair?' I stormed.

'He'd better watch his accusations,' said Mr Roy.

'It's time somebody stopped you treating us as if we're worthless.' I couldn't stop myself now, I was so incensed.

'Talk about bite the hand that feeds him,' Mr Roy puffed. 'Aren't I the one who gave him a job?'

'You can stick your job,' I hurled at him.

'Don't, Suresh,' my brother intervened.

'Don't what?' I said. 'Don't tell him that I'd rather go on the streets and beg than take his money? That I'd rather go home and be beaten by our father?'

'I'm not surprised his father beat him, ungrateful

233

brat. Get him out of here, Vikas, before I have him thrown out.'

'Don't bother,' I raged. 'I'll get myself out.'

'Thinks he calls the shots now,' the dealer sneered.

I pushed past Vikas and strode towards the door. It wouldn't budge when I tried to open it. I rattled it hard, then kicked it. Mr Roy came up behind me. 'Do that again and I won't be responsible for my actions,' he hissed into my ear. He slid past me, opened the door and directed me to leave. As I stalked past him and out into the pouring rain, followed by my brother, I heard him sneer, 'Good riddance to bad rubbish,' before slamming the door behind us. I kicked the door again for good measure, grabbed Sandeep's arm, and ran away before anyone came after us.

Chapter 23

'Now what are we going to do?' Sandeep asked as we traipsed through the streets. 'We've got nothing to eat again and no money to buy anything with.'

I didn't answer. I was still raging inside.

'We're worse off than ever now,' he grumbled. 'We can't even go back to our island.'

I shoved my hands deep into my pockets, hunched up my shoulders and quickened my pace, as if that would protect me from his complaints.

'Why did you have to pick a fight with him? He was no different today from any other day. I thought we decided it was better to be paid some money than nothing at all, even if he did always cheat us.'

If only the rain would stop. At least if it were dry we would know where we were sleeping that night. At least we wouldn't be wearing wet clothes that chafed our skin. We had waited so long for the arrival of the monsoon, yet within hours it had robbed us of our home and our job.

'We'll find someone better to work for,' I growled. 'Someone who treats us with a bit of respect.'

'Vikas says the dealers are all the same.'

'We'll find a different sort of work.'

'We tried that and nobody wanted us.'

'We'll have to try harder then.' I refused to be beaten, and I didn't want my brother going on and on and making me feel worse. Something would turn up, I was determined to believe that. I stopped in front of a shrine to Ganesh. Even the elephant god looked bedraggled, his silk drapes clinging limply.

We trudged on again. It was just like when we first arrived in the city, when we walked and walked with no particular place to go but hoping for some sort of inspiration. We had lived there for five months now, but we were worse off than when we arrived. Then, our clothes were smart, we had shoes on our feet, our skin was fresh and our eyes were sad but clear. Now, we looked like ragamuffins. Our clothes were torn and dirty. Our skin was scabby, scarred and burnt, our eyes red with hunger and lack of sleep.

'What about the railway station?' Sandeep suggested suddenly.

'Nobody'll give us a job there,' I grunted. 'Even if we could do it better than those two in our father's office.'

'I meant for somewhere to sleep,' Sandeep said, warming to his idea.

'They won't let us,' I said. 'They don't like people sleeping in there.'

'We can say it's while we're waiting for our train.'

'We can't say that every night.'

'They might let people while it's the monsoon. They might be kind because of that.'

I wondered if my brother might be right. After all, even the street dwellers who lived in doorways would have to move now that the storm drains were bursting and some of the roads were beginning to flood.

'OK,' I said, 'let's go and see.'

Sandeep was all eager then. He ran ahead of me, splashing his way along the deserted pavements. Now that the initial excitement over the monsoon had died down, people stayed under cover as much as possible, though the roads were still crawling with vehicles. But by the time we reached the station, the rain had slowed and the sun looked as if it was about to break through, which lifted my mood and made me feel as if something good might happen.

The station was packed. Some trains had been delayed because of the rain. People occupied every bench and every square foot of ground space, their luggage sprawled haphazardly, some of it doubling as seats, some as cots for exhausted babies. The noise was breathtaking, the atmosphere stifling. It took me back to the days when we visited Appa at his station office and looked down at the crowded concourse. Except that Appa's station had been a lot smaller and we had never been there during a monsoon. Here, it was as if the whole city had decided to catch a train at the same time.

'Nobody will ever know we're not travelling,' Sandeep shouted into my ear.

'There's no room to breathe,' I shouted back.

'Better than sleeping in a pond,' Sandeep grinned.

I wasn't so sure. Unless some trains came in to reduce the waiting crowd, I couldn't imagine being able to sleep at all, except perhaps upright against a wall, and even then the snorts and coughs and snuffles of hundreds of people would surely prevent it. We jostled our way through them in search of somewhere that might serve as a sleeping place that night.

A train was spotted in the distance at that moment and we found ourselves caught up in a sudden frenzy of pushing and shoving. I was pulled in one direction, Sandeep in another, until I lost sight of him completely. I yelled his name, but nobody could have made themselves heard in the pandemonium. I tried to fight my way out, but my head became a target for dozens of thrusting shoulders. A cry went up that another train was arriving. In an instant I was being carried in a new direction by another surge of bodies. There was nothing I could do but to wait until it came to a halt. I just prayed that it wouldn't deposit me on the tracks and that Sandeep was safe.

I freed myself finally when the station police called the crowd to order. I pushed my way through as they herded them to one side so that passengers already on the trains could dismount. Once I'd reached the back of the concourse I stood on a step and scanned the heads. I couldn't see Sandeep amongst them. Even when the numbers had thinned, I failed to find him. I began to worry that the police had seen him and recognised him as Arun's accomplice. Or that he had been unable to escape the pressing crowd and finished up on one of the trains. Or that he had decided to go home.

Two whistles blew almost simultaneously and the trains pulled slowly out of the station. I walked slowly round the edge of the concourse, and scoured the remaining faces. As I passed in front of a big pile of boxes, I heard my name.

'Suresh. Here, come here.'

I turned to see Sandeep beckoning me. He was sitting on the floor behind the boxes.

'What are you doing?' I hissed.

'I've found something. Come and see.'

I checked that nobody was looking then slid down on the floor next to him. 'What is it?' I asked.

'It's a wallet,' he whispered. He pulled it briefly from his pocket then pushed it back. 'It's got money in it, Suresh. Lots of it.'

'Where did you get it?'

'A man dropped it. He was running for the train and he dropped it. I tried to run after him but the crowds got in the way.'

I looked at him suspiciously and hated myself for it.

Where had my trust gone? 'We must give it back,' I said.

My brother's face dropped. 'We can't give it back,' he scoffed. 'The man's gone.'

'We'll have to find him,' I said simply.

'He's on a train, miles away.'

'I don't care,' I said. 'It doesn't belong to us.'

'It belongs to me,' Sandeep scowled. 'I found it and it's up to me what I do with it.'

'We've already had this discussion over the necklace.'

'That was different,' Sandeep argued. 'The necklace was stolen. The wallet has been lost and I've found it.'

'And if it's got that much money in it the owner will be desperate to get it back.' I looked him straight in the eyes. 'What happened to your morals?'

'They don't count any more,' he growled, though he couldn't hold my gaze. 'We're starving and there are thousands of rupees in that wallet and I don't see why we shouldn't have them because the man's probably rich. Anyway, what are you going to do? Hand it over to the police?'

Just for a moment I thought how much easier it would be to grab Sandeep's hand and run from the station. How much easier it would be to think that we were supposed to have that money and that was why my brother had found it. We deserved it, didn't we? The man wouldn't miss it, and anyway he shouldn't have been so careless as to lose it. How were we going to live if we didn't keep it?

'I'll have to hand it in,' I said.

'They'll think you stole it,' he sniffed. 'They'll put you in prison.'

'Has it got an address inside it?' I asked.

'What, so you can post it back? We can't even afford a stamp.'

'Give it to me and let me see.'

'No. You'll keep it.'

'Give it to me, Sandeep.'

I leant over and tried to pull it from his pocket. As he struggled to push me off him, a shadow fell across us.

'What are you two doing here?' A policeman hovered over us.

I jumped to my feet and pulled Sandeep up. 'We're waiting for a train, sir,' I said.

'Let me see your tickets.'

'We're waiting for someone to arrive on a train, sir,' Sandeep said quickly.

'Who are you meeting and where are they coming from?'

I wondered if we shouldn't just run, but if he caught us and found the wallet, that would be it. 'The truth is, sir, we were hoping to stay here until it's not so wet outside,' I said.

'That could be in three months' time,' the policeman replied, without smiling. 'In the meantime I've got a nice dry cell that's just perfect for street kids who cause a nuisance.'

'We won't be a nuisance, I promise. If we could just stay here tonight, and then we'll find somewhere else.'

He looked at us long and hard. Sandeep shifted anxiously, his hands stuffed deep into his pockets. He had guilt written all over his face.

'Don't let me catch you here again tomorrow,' he said at last. 'It's busy enough, without non-travellers adding to the chaos. And here, take this and get yourselves something to eat.'

He gave me four rupees and marched away before we could say anything else. I wished suddenly that I had told him about the wallet. He wouldn't have accused us of stealing it, I was sure. So far we had been lucky with our encounters with the police. The next time, if we took the wallet to a police station, we might not be so lucky.

We sat back down behind the boxes. Sandeep stuck his lip out defiantly, ready to fight back if I continued to insist that he give me the wallet. I asked him what he wanted to eat but he didn't answer. I wanted him to come with me to buy something. I was scared he might run away if I left him alone.

'Is there an address in the wallet?' I asked him for a second time. When he stubbornly refused to say a word, I said, 'If there's an address inside, we could take it back to the man.'

My brother looked at me as if I were completely mad. 'What, just turn up at his door and say, "Here's your wallet, sir"?'

'Yes.'

'What, and expect him to be grateful?'

'He won't be unhappy.'

'What if he thinks you took it in the first place because you thought you might get a reward when you returned it?'

'Why should he think that?'

'Because you're a street kid and everybody thinks street kids are bad.'

We fell silent again. I was adamant in my own mind that returning the wallet was the right thing to do. Sandeep was adamant that we should keep the money for ourselves, and I was sure he wouldn't give in even if I ordered him to hand the wallet over. Short of snatching it from him when he wasn't paying attention, I didn't know what to do. All I knew was that it lay in his pocket creating a damaging rift between us.

Chapter 24

We scarcely spoke a word to each other for the rest of that day. We bought ourselves something to eat from a pani-puri seller, then sat and waited for the crowds to die down so that we could sleep. The concourse cleared rapidly of travellers once the news spread that several trains had been cancelled because of flooding on the lines. I saw that we were not the only street dwellers to have sought shelter there. Whole families were camped out under rough blankets, some of them occupying the benches, others propped up against the perimeter walls.

Before we fell asleep, Sandeep looked me straight in the eyes and said, 'I'm going to buy us some new clothes and shoes tomorrow, whether you like it or not, and then we can find ourselves a good job.'

If only we could, I thought. How tempting the idea was.

I stared at his determined face. 'Think, Sandeep,' I said impatiently. 'If you go into a shop clutching enough money to buy all those things, they will have you arrested because they will believe that you stole the money. Can't you see what a bad thing for us this money is?'

'Then we will spend it bit by bit to buy ourselves food and somewhere to stay,' he said quickly.

'The food we buy with it will make us ill,' I sighed. I turned away from him. I didn't want to be tempted by what he was suggesting. I hardly dared close my eyes in case he vanished and I would never see him again, but I couldn't fight the exhaustion I felt.

When I woke, several hours later, I had a raging headache and felt horribly sick. Sandeep was snoring quietly beside me. I sat up and watched the station ragpickers go about their work, two policemen survey-ing them closely. My stomach churned. I stood and rushed to the toilets. It was several minutes before I felt safe enough to leave them. Rain was drumming loudly on the station roof, and the number of prostrate bodies on the ground had grown considerably since I had fallen asleep. I stared hard at my brother. He seemed to be in a deep sleep. I checked to see if the policemen were looking in the opposite direction. I leant across my brother, my palms sweating, and tried to slip a hand into his pocket. He moved and I withdrew it. I waited a few seconds to see what he would do, then had another go. I managed to catch the wallet between my first two fingers. I pulled carefully, little by little. At last I had it. I checked again that nobody was watching, before stuffing it in my own pocket. I stood up and walked back over to the toilets, checking once more that the policemen weren't watching. I didn't want them to think I was using the toilets to take drugs.

As soon as I had closed the door behind me, I took out the wallet and looked inside. I had never seen so much money. There were thousands of rupees. Sandeep was right. We could have lived happily for months on what was there. I felt the fatness of the notes, held the biggest one up to the light, sniffed a brand new one, ran one backwards and forwards through my fingers. Would it be so bad to keep just a few rupees?

I stuffed them back and searched for an address. There was a card with a man's details on it. For a moment I thought about screwing it up and throwing it away. I memorised it instead, put it back in the wallet, returned the wallet to my shorts, and went out. I made sure Sandeep was still asleep, then headed for the station entrance. I needed some air. The atmosphere inside the station was rank with a mixture of diesel fumes, smoke, stale vegetable oil and body odour. I pushed my way through the doors and stood out on the empty pavement.

Within seconds my still damp clothes were soaking. Water swirled round my ankles, carrying with it more of the city's waste. The nearby storm drains were overflowing. Several rickshaw-wallahs were dozing in their vehicles, waiting for their first passengers of the new day. One was awake and picking his nails. He tried to look more businesslike when I approached him, perhaps thinking that I might provide him with a fare, then went back to picking his nails when he recognised a street child beneath the sopping clothes.

'Do you know where Prithviraj Road is?' I asked him.

'I'll take you there,' he said instantly. 'Eighty rupees. I'm doing you a good deal. You have the money to pay?'

'I just wanted to know where it is,' I said, touching the wallet in my pocket.

'You don't want to go there?'

I shook my head and wondered why I felt so ill. 'Maybe later,' I said.

'Later will be too late I think,' the rickshaw-wallah grinned. 'If this rain continues, you'll need a boat.'

'Is it a long way?' I asked.

'Long way,' the man nodded. 'Right up behind the old palace in the new development. Posh area. You want to know the quickest route?'

'Please,' I said.

'Across the railway line and over the rubbish tip.' He laughed out loud and turned his back on me. I wished I could hire him then and there and wave a thousand rupees in front of his eyes when I finally allowed him to set me down.

I turned to go back into the station. The entrance seemed to blur as I walked towards it.

The pavement rose up with a rush of water which sucked my legs from beneath me. I vomited so hard that my guts felt as though they would rip. Voices tore at my head as the rain beat it to a pulp. I didn't know who I was any more or where I was. Rough hands tried to hold me. I fought them with all my might. They were trying to steal from me. I had nothing worth stealing. Were they trying to steal my soul? And then I clutched my pocket. I did have something worth stealing. I fought even harder. A scream came from somewhere inside my head. I remembered a name. Prithviraj Road. Number 14. I had to go there. I had to go there or be eaten alive. I began to shiver, so furiously I felt my bones would break. Something sharp attacked the top of my leg. I vomited again. A voice I thought I knew was calling from the other end of a long dark tunnel. Suresh, it whispered. Suuuurrreessssh.

A wave of calm swept across me. My head sank softly into a mountain of cotton wool. A hand closed itself round mine and squeezed.

Chapter 25

'Suresh.'

It was that voice again, but close by this time. I opened my eyes. Sandeep. It was Sandeep, looking down at me, terror written across his face. There were other faces too, faces I didn't know. One belonged to the policeman who had warned us to leave the station. I struggled to sit up but a strong hand pushed me back down.

'Steady there,' a man said. 'I'm a doctor. You have a bad bout of food poisoning, or possibly even malaria. I've given you an injection to stop you from becoming dehydrated, and you can take this medicine, but you should go to the hospital.'

I took the tablets and water that he held out to me and drank them down. I gazed again at the faces surrounding me. I had a reason to be scared of them, especially the policeman. What was that reason? I closed my eyes and tried to work out what had happened. And then I remembered.

'I feel better now,' I said, attempting again to sit up. 'My brother will look after me.'

'You may have another attack,' the doctor warned. 'I have time to ring for an ambulance before I catch my train.'

'I'll be fine,' I said adamantly. All I could think about was that the policeman was hovering over me while I had a wallet full of money in my pocket. The idea of being taken to hospital appalled me. They might telephone my father to take me home. They might take Sandeep away from me. They might discover the wallet and lock me up. I summoned all my strength, took Sandeep by the hand and stood up.

'I'm all right,' I aimed at the doctor, though my head was spinning and I badly needed to find the toilets.

'Well, I can't force you,' the doctor said. 'And I can't spend any more time trying to persuade you to be sensible.'

He picked up his briefcase and strode into the station. The crowd that had gathered round me began to disperse. The policeman stared at me and was about to say something, when I just had to go.

'I need –' I started to explain, then dashed into the station to find the toilets. While I squatted there, I hoped that the policeman wouldn't think I was running away from him. I heard the door open.

'Suresh? Are you all right, Suresh?'

'I'll be all right soon,' I attempted to reassure my brother.

'The wallet's gone, Suresh. Someone's taken the wallet.'

'Shhh!' I hissed. 'Wait till I come out.'

I heard the door open again. 'How is he?' a voice asked.

'I'm fine,' I called out. 'Absolutely fine.'

'If you need to stop here another night you can, but then you should go home. Understood?'

I heard Sandeep mutter, 'Yes, sir,' while I wondered vaguely if I was being given permission to stop in the toilet.

'Sorry about the food poisoning, if that's what it is.'

The door slammed shut. There was a moment's silence before Sandeep said, 'You can come out. He's gone.'

I wasn't sure how safe I was to leave, but we needed to be on our way. I tried to ignore my gurgling stomach and went out of the cubicle. Sandeep threw himself at me. He was close to tears. I realised how scared he had been. I took him by the shoulder and led him back out on to the concourse, across to the entrance.

As soon as we were outside, I said quietly to him, 'I've got the wallet. I took it to find the address. We're going to go there now and hand it back before the police find it on us.'

My brother didn't argue. Even if he still thought we should keep it, he knew it was too dangerous. I think he understood, too, that he would have to fight me to get the wallet back. We set off through the city as it began to wake up to another day of monsoon. I kept an eye out for our friends but failed to spot any of them. Perhaps they had decided that digging through the mushy mess of refuse that perished outside shops and houses before slithering into the drainage system was too much trouble for the few rupees they would earn. I felt sorry for those who collected waste paper. If the rain kept on, they would struggle for weeks to find anything worth salvaging. The shoe-shine boys would find it hard as well. They wouldn't be able to shine shoes in the rain. Even the garland-makers would have a difficult time. Much of the blossom would be destroyed. At least Vikas and Chintu would still be able to pick up aluminium cans, as long as they weren't all swept away by floods.

I walked faster, though my head pounded with every step. In places the water came halfway up our calves. Whenever a taxi went by it soaked us. Sandeep thought it was funny, but I was too tired to join in when he attempted a water fight. It would have been exhausting enough to walk to the new suburbs if the streets were clear. It was doubly hard wading through the floods. By the time we reached the alleyways that led to the slums I was ready to give up. They were so narrow that there were no storm drains. Accumulated rubbish was spread across them and wrapped itself round our feet as we trawled our way through.

'Is this the only way to get there?' Sandeep asked, pulling at a plastic bag that had attached itself to his ankle.

'The rickshaw-wallah said it would take hours to go round.'

'Couldn't we at least have used a bit of the money to get a taxi to go there, especially since you're not well? It's because he lost the wallet in the first place that we're having to do this.'

I couldn't answer. Sandeep had a good point, but it

still didn't seem right to use someone else's money without their permission.

'You're so stubborn, Suresh,' he grumbled.

'Perhaps they'll pay for us to get a taxi back,' I said.

'They better had. It's the least they can do.'

I thought about the days when we used to get a taxi into town and back again with Amma. It seemed such a long time ago. Even if we went home, nothing would ever be the same again. We had been through so much. Trips to town would have no meaning any more. We had had our bellyful of gazing into shop windows knowing that everything we saw was beyond our pockets and always would be. We had had to grow up too quickly.

We reached the end of the alleyways and headed on to the wasteland in front of the slums. I was more shocked than ever by what I saw there. The ground was completely waterlogged and had turned into a mud bowl. The slums themselves had been so battered by the rains that some of those that I could see had collapsed altogether, while others had lost their flimsy palm or tarpaulin roofs. Mud and water from the wasteland had flowed down through the main street, leaving filthy deposits outside the houses, through which young children were crawling. Behind the railway line, the rubbish tip rose like a giant boil. There were crowds of people on it, drawn there because in the monsoon rains it was increasingly impossible to earn a living on the streets. We crossed the wasteland, pushed our way through the hedge, and began to climb up the side. Even as we did, I found myself, out of habit, looking out for pieces of glass.

The effort of climbing up the tip was almost too much for me. The smell was terrible and made me want to vomit all over again. For every step forward that we took, we slid back half a step on the slimy surface. I had to sit down and catch my breath when we were only halfway up. I scoured the faces of the children close by. To my delight I saw that one of them was Chintu, and not far away from him was Tej. I waved to Chintu when he stood up to stretch. He came over.

'I heard what happened with Mr Roy,' he said. 'That man is no good. What will you do now?'

'I don't know yet,' I said, 'but we've got to go and see someone first.'

'For a job?' he asked.

I shook my head, but didn't offer any explanation.

'Are you going to the party tonight?' he asked.

'We're not going to let the monsoon stop us, are we, Tej? We'll have a water party.'

I watched Sandeep's face light up for the first time that day. 'We wouldn't miss it,' I grinned.

'Are you all right?' Chintu said, looking at me carefully.

'A bit of food poisoning, that's all,' I told him. 'Anyway, we'd better be off. See you later.'

'If you need any money for food,' Chintu called after us, 'you only have to ask. I've got some savings. And Tej says he'll help.'

'Thanks, Chintu. Thanks, Tej.'

We set off again. When we reached the top, we paused to look at the view. We had never ventured into the suburbs. As far as we could see there were very few shops and offices, and the houses seemed to be less crammed together. I picked out what must have been the old palace. Behind it the houses looked new and a lot of building work was going on round them.

'That must be where we've got to go,' I said to Sandeep. 'The rickshaw-wallah said it was in the new part.' We stayed there for a few moments longer. It was somehow liberating to stand in the torrential rain and look out across the rooftops. Then we part walked, part slid down the other side, before having to cross a pool of water that had accumulated at the bottom.

'They'll get a shock when we turn up at their door,' Sandeep chuckled, 'especially looking like this.'

'And especially when we hand them the wallet,' I joined in.

'What if nobody answers?' Sandeep asked.

I hadn't wanted to think about that. In my mind we would knock on the door and somebody would answer and I would pull the wallet from my pocket – like magic – and they would be so happy and grateful and perhaps they might offer us something to eat if they were kind.

'We'll have to wait,' I said. I couldn't conceive of going away with the wallet still in our possession and returning another day.

'We might miss the party,' my brother grumbled. 'And what if they don't come back tonight?'

'Let's just hope they do,' I said, irritable now.

We headed in the general direction of the old palace. I was so tired, hungry and thirsty. My stomach felt as though it had been put through a mangle, while the thumping in my head made me feel sick all over again. I longed to lie down and go to sleep and promised myself that that was what I would do as soon as we returned to the city centre, party or no party. We made our way through a network of streets, all of which were much cleaner than the ones we were used to. I wondered if there was any work in the area for ragpickers and, if so, who their dealer was. I wondered if they allowed people to sleep in the streets. I was aware that we were attracting a lot of attention, probably because we were strangers, but also because nobody else looked as shabby and dirty as we did. I hurried Sandeep along. I felt uncomfortable and was keen to get back to the city centre as quickly as possible.

Chapter 26

It was still some time before we arrived at Prithviraj Road. We took several wrong turns before we finally found ourselves at one end of a street which was lined with two-storey houses, each of them a different design and with a gated paved area in front. Sandeep and I stared down the street, stared at each other, then stared down the street again. I noticed that even though it was teeming with rain, the drains were coping with the downpour and there was no flooding.

'This is it,' I said, pointing at the road sign.

'Prithviraj Road,' said Sandeep.

'Number 14 must be somewhere in the middle.'

'They must have lots of money, the people who live here,' my brother observed.

I began to feel nervous at the prospect of approaching the house and knocking on the door. It would have taken very little to make me turn on my heel and run, though I scarcely had any energy left to walk.

'Which side do you think it's on?' Sandeep asked.

'Left,' I said.

'I bet right,' he grinned.

'I bet you're wrong.' I forced myself into action. We walked slowly along, gazing into each house in turn, wondering if someone might dash out and demand to know what we were doing. When we reached number 14, which was on the left, I was so tense that my legs started to shake.

'Are we going in?' asked Sandeep.

'In a minute.'

'What are you going to say?'

'I'm going to say, "We're sorry to disturb you but we're looking for Mr Dixit."'

'And then what?'

A face appeared at a window of the house. A woman's face. Moments later, the front door opened. Sandeep grabbed my elbow and stood behind me.

'Was there something you wanted?' the woman said.

I held on to the gatepost for support. 'We're looking for Mr Dixit.' My voice was little more than a whisper.

'And why would you want Mr Dixit?' The woman stared at us searchingly.

'Does he live here?' I didn't want to tell her about the wallet without being sure that we were at the right place.

'I am Mrs Dixit,' the woman said. I couldn't decide if she was friendly or not. She might have been scared of us. She was certainly cautious. She didn't leave her doorstep, but I could see that she was beautifully dressed and younger than Amma.

'I don't know what business you have with my husband,' she continued, 'but he is away until this evening.'

I decided that I would have to trust her. I took a deep breath and blurted out, 'We found his wallet, Mrs Dixit.'

'*I* found his wallet,' Sandeep said firmly. 'He dropped it in the station and he was gone before I could give it back to him.'

It took a moment for the information to sink in. Mrs Dixit seemed to weigh up what we said, then stepped forward from the shelter of her doorway. 'Can I see it?' she said.

I opened the gate carefully, not wanting to damage it, and walked up the path towards her. I pulled the wallet from my pocket and held it out to her. She stretched out her hand to take it. She turned it over then looked inside. I saw her raise her eyebrows when she felt the money.

'It's all there,' I said quickly. 'We haven't taken any of it, not even to get here. We wouldn't do that, would we, Sandeep?'

'We wouldn't do that,' Sandeep agreed.

She stared hard at us, then at last her face broke into a smile. 'You are very honest boys,' she said, 'and your honesty deserves a reward.'

Sandeep nudged me from behind.

'Come inside and you shall have something to eat,' she said.

I gazed down at my soaking wet, filthy clothes and my bare feet and wondered how I could possibly accept her invitation.

'I wouldn't dream of letting you go without feeding you at least,' Mrs Dixit insisted. 'Now come inside. I think you might enjoy a nice hot shower as well, am I right?'

Sandeep and I both nodded shyly, but were scarcely able to contain our excitement. It wasn't just the offer of food, but we had never had a hot shower before.

'This way, then,' encouraged Mrs Dixit. 'My house-keeper will find you some big towels and we can even wash and dry your clothes for you while you have something to eat.'

'Go on, Suresh,' said my brother.

'I promise I won't bite,' Mrs Dixit laughed.

The offer of food and a shower was too much. I allowed myself to be led through the doorway, Sandeep at first following close behind me but then pushing in front as soon as we walked into a beautifully decorated hall.

'Wow!' he breathed. 'I've never been in anywhere as nice as this.'

'We like it,' Mrs Dixit smiled. 'And it's not so very grand.'

'It is when you've been living on a traffic island,' Sandeep blurted out.

I glared at him crossly. I didn't want her to know things like that about us.

'A traffic island!' she exclaimed.

'It was the best place. All our friends told us that,' said Sandeep.

'It was all right until the monsoon started,' I said.

'Well, let's get you showered and then you can tell me all about it,' she said. She rang a bell and from somewhere in the house an old woman appeared, who looked us up and down with undisguised disapproval. 'I'd like you to show our guests into the bathroom and find them some towels and bathrobes. And please, Mrs Karki, would you take their clothes and wash and dry them.'

We had the best shower we had ever had in our lives. We scrubbed away with the soap and shampoo, determined to get rid of every last grain of dirt, grime and sweat. The water that ran away across the floor was a thick grey. I felt so much better when I was clean. It was as if I had washed away all the worries and fears, the sickness and exhaustion. After we had dried ourselves with the soft white towels, we wrapped ourselves in the silky bathrobes. Sandeep giggled and said we had turned into posh people with the scrub of a brush. We unlocked the bathroom door and crept out into the hallway. Another door opened immediately. Mrs Dixit welcomed us into the kitchen, telling us to sit at the table and make ourselves at home. She put a pile of bhajis and samosas in front of us and told us to eat. It was the most food we had seen since we left home. Sandeep grabbed at it and stuffed himself silly. Mrs Dixit sat watching him, amused, I think, by his obvious enjoyment of the meal. 'Save some room for the vegetable biriani,' she said when we had virtually cleared the plate. We were astonished to learn that there was more to come. My stomach was protesting already, partly because it was upset but also because it couldn't cope with this quantity of food.

Quietly and gently, Mrs Dixit questioned us about where we were from and why we were living on the streets. I was reluctant to answer, afraid that her questions might be a trap and that she might have ideas about sending us home. I told her as much as I could, but I didn't reveal the village where we came from, and I pretended that we had lots of people to look after us in the city. She asked if we could read and write. Sandeep jumped in and said that we had been to a very good school and could read and write very well.

'Don't you miss going to school?' she asked.

'Sometimes,' I said. 'And I'm scared that I won't ever get a good job because I left school early. And I'm scared for Sandeep because he needs to be at school now.'

My brother pulled a face. Mrs Dixit smiled. She gazed at me long and hard. 'My husband needs an office boy,' she said at last. She waited for my reaction. I sat up straight and bit my lip. 'He needs someone honest and willing,' she continued. I nodded my head. 'It's difficult to tell whether people are honest or not until you know them quite well,' she added. 'My housekeeper thinks I am mad to have you in the house. She thinks the minute my back is turned you'll steal my silver.'

I was astonished when she said that. I knew the housekeeper disapproved of us because of the way we looked, but it had not occurred to me that she might doubt our honesty.

'But we brought Mr Dixit's wallet back,' Sandeep protested.

Mrs Dixit smiled again. 'And that is why I am going to suggest that he talk to your brother about the job.'

I thought I was hearing things. 'Talk to me?' I said. 'But I'm just a street kid.'

'You are a child who, for no fault of his own, has had no choice other than to live on the streets.'

'It's the same for most of the children who live on the streets,' I said.

'You are the one who landed on my doorstep clutching my husband's wallet, and my husband only has room for one office boy,' she replied.

'What about me?' complained Sandeep. 'I was the one who found the wallet.'

'I would like to help you go back to school.'

My brother pulled a face again. 'School's boring,' he said.

'And picking through people's rubbish is fun?' Mrs Dixit raised her eyebrows. 'You surprise me.'

I was glad to have her support. It was difficult for Sandeep to argue with an adult.

We were interrupted by the housekeeper, who reappeared with our freshly washed and ironed clothes. I was amazed that they were dry. Mrs Dixit saw my face. 'That's where tumble dryers are invaluable,' she smiled. 'Especially when it's too wet to hang things outside to dry.'

We went off to get dressed. 'We'd look really smart if we had shoes as well,' I said to Sandeep. Our clothes looked so nice, even if they were very worn.

'If you get the job we'll be able to afford shoes,' said Sandeep. 'I'm not going to any boring old school without them.'

'Let's just see what happens,' I replied.

Mrs Dixit agreed that we were very presentable when we returned to the kitchen. 'I'll order you a taxi back into the city,' she said. 'When my husband returns, I will tell him all about you. I want you to meet with him at this address tomorrow at midday.

It's in the centre. Do you think you'll be able to find it?'

I nodded and thanked her several times.

'It's for me to thank you,' she said. 'My husband will be eternally grateful to you.'

Chapter 27

The taxi ride was such a relief. I had dreaded going back over the tip. I could barely keep my eyes open. It seemed like many hours had passed since I had collapsed in the station, yet it was still the same day. I tried to stop my mind from jumping ahead, from celebrating the fact that I would soon have a new job, a job I could be proud of. Sandeep sat beside me, full of talk about the house we had just visited and about how our life would change when I had a proper job. He didn't want to go back to school, but if the choice was between ragpicking and school, he would choose school. He was determined that we should go to the party that night. I was worried about it. I didn't know how my friends would react to the possibility that I might have a better job. Sandeep argued that we had told Chintu we were going and that Chintu would be disappointed if we didn't. In the end I agreed, provided that he kept quiet about the job.

'It'll be embarrassing if we tell everybody about it and then Mr Dixit turns me down,' I said.

'I won't say anything,' Sandeep promised, 'as long as you promise we can go.'

We asked the taxi driver to drop us off by Bharat's stall. Our friend's face was a picture when he saw us get out of the taxi, our hair clean, our clothes neat and tidy. We sat down with him for a few moments before he closed his stall. He was keen for us to help ourselves to a pile of puris that he had left over. For once, we weren't hungry, but I didn't want to upset him and took one anyway. We told him about the wallet and what had happened to us that day. I didn't mind that he knew about my prospect of a job. It wasn't like telling my friends, who might feel that we were deserting them. Bharat considered what we said and nodded his head.

'Many people would not have returned the wallet,' he said. 'Even I might have thought twice about it. You will have your reward for doing the right thing. Do you remember what my friend the fortune teller told you?'

I remembered. 'He said, "Your luck is round the corner".'

'One makes one's own luck, and you have made yours,' said Bharat. 'Believe my friend, and you shall have your job. I will be the first to clap my hands and say thank you to the gods. '

'We'll be able to pay for our puris if Suresh gets the job,' said Sandeep.

'I will never allow that,' smiled Bharat. 'Even if he becomes the richest man in India.'

It was too early to go to the party. The rain was slowing to a drizzle, and I had an urge to visit our island. We walked along the streets and watched the shopkeepers closing for the night. We didn't try to hide in the shadows. We were smart enough, we thought, to hold our heads up high. Just for fun, we gazed in through some of the shop windows and pointed out what we would buy if we had enough money.

When we reached the demolished building, we stood in the rubble and looked across at our island. In the growing darkness, we were happy to see that nobody else had claimed it.

'It's safe until the monsoon is over,' I said quietly to Sandeep.

'Will we go back there then?' he asked.

'Who knows where we'll be then,' I said.

'We might be living in a house like Mrs Dixit's,' laughed Sandeep.

'That's one dream too far,' I smiled. 'But perhaps we might have found somewhere where there's shelter.'

'Will we mind if somebody else takes our island?'

'I don't think we will if we've found somewhere better.'

'Will we write to Amma then?'

'Yes, we'll write to Amma.'

We left our rubble hideout and walked back through the streets towards the tannery. On the way, we made one last detour. I followed the directions Mrs Dixit had given me until we found ourselves outside the building where I was to meet her husband. We stood outside and looked up at it.

'It's posh, isn't it?' whispered Sandeep.

I nodded. 'Your luck is round the corner,' I repeated to myself.

'No more broken glass?' Sandeep said.

I ruffled his hair. 'No more broken glass.'

Sally Grindley

Sally Grindley lives in Cheltenham and has worked in children's books all her career – first as an editor for a children's book club and then as a full-time writer. Sally is the author of many outstanding books for young readers. She is the winner of a Smarties Prize gold award for *Spilled Water*. Sally travels extensively to research her novels. Her other novels for Bloomsbury are *Feather Wars*, *Hurricane Wills* and *Saving Finnegan*.